C

Bone

D0400935

Also by Nance Van Winckel

The 24 Doors: Advent Calendar Poems (Minneapolis:
Bieler Press, 1985)

Bad Girl, with Hawk (Urbana: University of Illinois
Press, 1988)

The Dirt: Poems (Oxford, Ohio: Miami University
Press, 1994)

Limited Lifetime Warranty: Stories (Columbia:
University of Missouri Press, 1994)

Quake: Stories (Columbia: University of Missouri
Press, 1997)

After a Spell: Poems (Oxford, Ohio: Miami University
Press, 1998)

Curtain Creek Farm: Stories (New York: Persea Books,
2000)

Beside Ourselves: Poems (Oxford, Ohio: Miami
University Press, 2003)

No Starling: Poems (Seattle: University of Washington
Press, 2007)

Pacific Walkers: Poems (Seattle: University of
Washington Press, 2013)

⑥

Boneland
Linked Stories

Nance Van Winckel

UNIVERSITY OF OKLAHOMA PRESS : NORMAN

Publication of this book is made possible through the generosity of
Edith Kinney Gaylord.

Library of Congress Cataloging-in-Publication Data

Winckel, Nance Van.
  [Short stories. Selections]
  Boneland : linked stories / Nance Van Winckel.
    pages ; cm.
  ISBN 978-0-8061-4391-0
  I. Winckel, Nance Van. Feeling like something's in the eye: Lynette,
age 40, 1997.   II. Title.
  PS3572.A546B66 2013
  813'.54—dc23
                                                        2013007082

Demeter to the Princes of Eleusis

There are mysteries no one may utter,
for deep ache checks the tongue.
Blessed is he who has seen them;
his lot will be good in the world to come.

Contents

Boneland

A Feeling Like Something's in the Eye

Lynette, age 40, 1997

Across from the B. C. Eye Clinic is the Willow Motel. An orderly walks you back to your room when the surgery's over. He opens your door, and if you answer yes, you'd like some sound, he turns on the TV or the radio. He'll get you a cup of tea, or a Coke. He'll leave you a pager, first placing your fingers over a special button so you can feel the bump there of a piece of tape. Just press that, and he'll be back in a flash.

And so all one's needs are met.

Lie back now, Miss Lynette. Rest, he says.

I was coming awake in British Columbia, and there was snow coming down. Or maybe there was only a mirage of snow, since my sight those days wasn't to be trusted. I was seeing starbursts. Earlier I'd seen halos around the heads of the horrible motel dogs and the unctuous orderly.

That's completely as it should be, the orderly says. That's par for the course.

Up Highway 1A is the Kokanee Glacier. Ten million years ago it got this far south and west and gave up. I've walked on it. Stood on the Precambrian rubble. Frozen scat from woolly mammoths. Extinct berries. Amid this primeval trash are lime Jell-O boxes, red rubber bands, and a Teenage Mutant Ninja Turtle whose legs are pinned in the ice but whose arms seem to struggle upward, reaching out stubby teenage ninja hands. All this under my feet. Under the murky frozen crust and a hot noontime sun.

The orderly suggests more drops for my eyes. Tears, he calls them. Artificial tears.
Is there snow? I ask. Real snow?
Isn't it weird? It's nearly May.
How will I drive back to Washington?
What driving? he says. Surely you jest.

I try to make my breathing slow down. Try to push back at all that crowds in to suggest what may soon no longer be seen. The list assembles itself up one motel room wall, then spills across another: *Ice On The Walk, On The Curb. My Cousin Buster Spinning On The Ice In His Black Skates. The Ferry Coming In. Trees Slumped Under Snow. What's In My Salad? What's In My Stew? Hairdos, Streetlights, Mold On The Cheese, The Rattlesnake Ring Through My Cousin Jessie's Navel. The Ferry Going Out. Sparks, Copper Cookie Cutters, Tools In The Tool Chest, A Man's Hands As They Reach For Me. Wild Onions Shooting Up Near The Aspens. The Aspens.*

The orderly knocking. The orderly's spiels. Another Coke? More sugar in that tea? And don't, under any circumstances, rub your eyes. The orderly going away.

The laser's pulse had made a ticking sound when it hit my eye. Then the smell like hair burning. The doctor's voice as if coming from inside a metal pipe. The microkeratome is just cutting a flap. Now we're folding the flap back. Now we're remaking the flap. Just keep looking directly at the blinking light.

In the motel, I'm awakened by the cry of an animal. A dog, I think. It's hurt. Its agony is a high vowel lapping at the room. My heart loudly running away with itself. The dog's stepped into a trap. I've heard such stories up here in Canada. The traps are set for the wolves. Any dog who steps in one is considered too stupid to save.

Do not, repeat, do *not* rub your eyes.

If I am unable, next week or next month, to see the glacier, am I simply to stand there in memory? With memory? Memory grows sharper, brighter. That's what the sightless are told by the sighted. In one memory my Uncle Mel hands me the petrified bony eye socket of a who-knows-what that's been dead for a few million years. He holds it down so I can touch it. I see that he's put inside the bone cavity a glass eye, a lavender iris. Someone's painted tiny red veins onto the white part. Uncle Mel laughs and gives me the eye to keep. Where is it now?

The dog steps out of the trap and limps toward the glacial sludge, sips at its edges, tastes an extinct berry. Sharper now. A brighter red: that gnawed place where his paw used to be.

In the parking lot Waylon Jennings drifts out from someone's truck when the door's thrown open. Down his voice, America slides into Canada.

Lie back now and rest. Here's the button. Here's your tea.

5

Did the dog live? He was most unwise to eat that berry. The berry made him lie down. Perhaps it was a short nap that turned into a wild, raucous sleep. Maybe the dream became his demise. Spokane, my town, seems so far away. So far. I lie back. Now the cold brightens. Now the cold gathers more cold; it gathers more everything into its glittering glacial freeze.

The Rage of the Bipedal

Lynette, age 12, 1969

"You won't feel anything," Lynette's mother told her. "They'll put you to sleep."

"Yeah," her brother Robert said, "like they do dogs."

He was fourteen, two years older, and he was supposed to be helping. The glare their mother leveled at him was intended to remind him of that.

But Robert didn't see the look. Bent over his plate, he was pushing julienned carrots away from Brussels sprouts. Any carrots that hadn't touched the sprouts, he'd eat.

"What if I wake up dead?" Lynette tossed her napkin on her plate. She knew something that had gone too long unsaid had finally slipped out.

Robert's head rose. He glared at her. "You don't wake up if you're dead, Lynnie."

"Duh-uh, that's exactly what I'm saying." Even to her own ears, her voice sounded loud. She felt herself maybe only fifteen or twenty seconds away from the quivery chin and sobbed-out sentences. She hated herself in that state.

"Dr. Issandi's performed thirty-seven of these operations, and she's never lost a patient," her mother said.

Yet, Lynette was tempted to add.

Her mother liked to emphasize the word *performed*, as if Dr. Issandi were a famous pianist playing at the Opera House. "You ought to have more faith." Her mother smiled, which only expanded her already oversized nostrils. Lynette had that same nose. They'd both gotten it, according to her father, from her mother's mother, Grandmother Rose. *Rose the Nose*, he'd say, and laugh—although not when her mother was in the room.

Ugh was what Lynette was thinking: about the nose and about the need for more faith.

"Do we have to talk about this while we're eating?" Robert asked, though Lynette knew that the discussions of her scapular height and realigned ligaments were, for him, more boring than unappetizing.

Their mother set her knife down loudly on her plate. "She *needs* to talk about it, Robert. Who wouldn't?"

"The world's a lot bigger than Lynnie's back," he said.

"Look, what you don't get, young man, is that you're just lucky. It could have been you." Their mother leaned toward him. "Are you following me?"

Holding their mother's eyes, he inched his plate slowly toward the center of the table. There were still four Brussels sprouts on it, but because the discussion had turned so serious, Lynette knew—and she knew that Robert knew—their mother wouldn't make an issue of the uncleaned plate.

Then he looked at Lynette. "You'll get to miss Scout camp," he said, his face as calm as an icy little lake.

"*What?*" Their mother turned to Lynette, then quickly back to Robert. "She likes camp." Her face had that look of having been slapped, but not hard. There was so much their mother simply assumed, blindly accepted. Her eyes were wide, bulging with white, brimming with faith.

"It's *my* back," Lynette said for the umpteenth time. "One little slip and I'm worm food. Like little Nickki Martin. Or worse, I'll be a vegetable and lie around all day sipping hotdog juice from a straw." She felt herself warding off tears with anger. She'd been doing that a lot lately and was good at it now. Next she would have to push her chair back, stand as straight as possible, and storm out of the kitchen. Which is just what she did.

"Thanks a lot," she heard her mother say to Robert.

Passing through the living room, Lynette felt her rigid back revert to its usual state: the humped, crooked old woman's. She stood at the bottom of the stairs. The seventeen steps involved precise quantities of pain, and she took a long breath, eyeing the top.

"She looks up to you," their mother was telling Robert, which was one more lie she'd chosen, long ago, to believe.

"I'm not drying all those pans," her brother said in the kitchen.

"Of course not," their mother answered. "I wouldn't want you to do anything that's not, strictly speaking, your job."

Dr. Issandi had a tiny diamond in her left nostril. At their first meeting, Lynette guessed that a bit of glitter must have fallen on Dr. Issandi from the Christmas tree in the medical center lobby. Lynette had never seen anyone her mother's age with anything pierced but ear lobes.

The diamond was subtle and delicate, like Dr. Issandi's nose itself. And once—maybe on the fourth or fifth visit—Lynette had said how much she admired the diamond. "It looks nice on you," she'd said, although she only wanted to steer their talk to something other than spines.

"I've had it since I was a baby," Dr. Issandi said. "I don't even know it's there anymore."

"A thing like that would just make my big old honker look bigger," Lynette said. Lying across her lap was an example of the sort of titanium rod Dr. Issandi wanted to run up either side of Lynette's spine. It looked like something that should go inside a furnace.

"You have a good nose." Dr. Issandi put her cool fingers against Lynette's nose. "It's rather noble, really."

"I hate it," Lynette said, recalling the chart of evolution that had stretched above Mr. Kraus's blackboard last year in fifth grade science. On the chart, fish rose out of the water and morphed into monstrous birds, which in turn morphed into dinosaurs, while the apes lost their hair and slowly—at the far right end of the millennia—stooped and then stood upright, having donned shirts and ties. Lynette had heard Heather Rollins tell someone that Lynette's nose looked like that ape boy's, the one who sat crouched over a tiny red fire.

"Lean forward." Dr. Issandi pressed on each of Lynette's vertebrae, nodding and speaking about herself as a team: "we've never lost a patient; we have a perfect record." Her diamond flashed. Years ago her family had been persecuted in Pakistan. But here in America, their lives had turned out beautifully.

"I feel quite sure," she said, "all shall be fine in the end."

Passing her parents' bedroom door, Lynette heard her mother's voice—not the soft one she used on the phone with Aunt Dot to talk about their sister-in-law Mary, but the louder, throatier voice she used with her father. He'd be speaking—practically shouting, really—from the radio phone on a ship in the middle of the Bering Sea. Her father had made it clear before he left that there was a mission to be accomplished during his three months away on the *Eugenia.* Lynette should be signed off on it. Dr. Issandi didn't want to perform on an unwilling patient. In five more weeks, the *Eugenia* would be full of salmon and Lynette's father would be back home in Spokane, whistling from room to room, expecting everything to be shipshape, and Lynette to be primed for a little snip-snip-snip.

Back in her room, she put her headphones on. The tape player's batteries were low, and a Fat Nothing song groaned. She guessed that her mother had told her father how again today Robert and Lynette had been too much, and no doubt her father had complained about the rough seas and the ignorant new guys, and then said he was sure the too-muchness of the kids was nothing she couldn't handle. In the photograph over Lynette's desk, her father, wearing yellow oilers, dangled in his harness above a deck that glistened with ice, the water in the background pure black. Without the harness connecting him from his belt to the mast, her father would have been— and many times, he's told her—swept overboard. "Though you'd have a heart attack from the cold before you'd have time to drown," he always added, grinning as if that were a joke among fishermen.

The Fat Nothing tape sputtered to grunts at the end. When Lynette took off the headphones and stepped into the hall-way, the house had gone dark—no lines of light beneath her brother's door, or her mother's. Everyone was tired. Tired of thinking. Tired of trying. Tired of being tired.

Later, in her dream, the wings she's sprouted are somehow recognizable—as though she's dreamed this before, or maybe lived this before. The wings flap but don't lift her high enough to catch a strong updraft. She curses them. She's not surprised she knows how to fly, only that for all her effort, she's getting nowhere. Up ahead are other winged people, and like them, she's supposed to toss a gold coin into a china bowl when she passes it—*if* she can ever get there. Then she'll be permitted entry. To *where* is unclear. But it seems to be the place everyone's going—all laughing and crowding in. There's a steady tink, tink, tink as gold coins drop, which—as Lynette turns over, awake and blinking—she realizes is her radiator filling with hot water.

Lynette's cousin Jessie had hammered a nail into her Barbie Angie—right through the lip—and was using the hammer's claw to yank the nail out. Jessie said she was going to put an earring—a gold hoop—in the lip's hole. Lynette's own Barbie, Midge—with wild snarled hair and a nail protruding from her left breast—looked like a vampire whose heart had had a stake driven through it.

Lynette and Jessie had brought their old Barbies out to the back porch at Aunt Dot and Uncle Mel's place. The Barbarians, they called the dolls. Jessie said it was time to make them modern women. Jessie had been her cousin for only three years, but it seemed longer. It seemed like forever. They'd stripped off the dolls' ball gowns and tiny high heels and were using Uncle Mel's taxidermy tools to perform the piercings. The Barbies were surprisingly tough.

"Remember how little Nickki loved to play Barbie?" Lynette asked Jessie. Little Nickki had been on her mind a lot lately.

Jessie nodded and pushed her dark bangs back. "Pass me those pliers." She was having trouble getting the nail out of Angie's lip.

Nickki Martin had gotten as far as the fifth grade with them. Then one January morning in 1967, her whole family had been obliterated by a logging truck. *Blindsided* was the word people used. The truck had skidded on a downhill curve—not "negotiating" it, Lynette's father had remarked. Later, everyone said how the truck driver was to be pitied, not condemned. He'd climbed out of his cab and waded into the wreckage, then radioed for help. The state troopers had to use the jaws of life to get to the Martins, although there was no life left in that car. This was all covered in graphic detail in the newspaper, which Lynette's mother had read aloud in their kitchen, right after the headlines about the three astronauts who'd burned to death inside their command module at Cape Kennedy.

There were three things Lynette remembered from that time two years ago. One was the word everyone in her class kept repeating, a word none of them had ever heard used in the context of the twentieth century: *decapitation.* Each time someone said it, its visual clarity seemed to sharpen in their minds.

The second thing was *That mud on the roadside wasn't mud, buddy; it was blood. Get real.* Lynette had overheard a state trooper say this to a security guard, and now she had no idea why such a sentence uttered in the mall parking lot had stuck so hard in her mind.

The last thing, of course, was little Nickki's funeral, and how she and Jessie had clung to each other all the way up to the casket, which in her memory was pink, but may have only had a pink lining. She'd grown less sure about that. "What in the world?" Aunt Dot had said to Lynette's mother. Apparently no one expected the caskets to be open: two in one room and three in another. But Lynette and Jessie only had to "pay their respects" to the one. Nickki wore a lacey, high-collared white blouse. Someone had put a pale peach lipstick on her, which struck Lynette as something Nickki's mother wouldn't have liked . . . until she recalled that Nickki's mother was in a box across the hall. Later, she and Jessie would agree that the high collar did nothing to hide what was underneath—those tan stitches zigzagging around little Nickki's throat. It was like seeing trees through gauze curtains.

"Remember those dorky white gloves they made Nickki wear?" Jessie asked. The gold hoop she'd finally maneuvered into Barbie Angie's lip looked like a giant noodle the doll was trying to suck into her mouth.

Lynette had given up nailing the silver earring post into Barbie Midge's breast and had put a bubble of rubber cement over the nail hole. "Really stupid and gross stuff can happen when you die," she told Jessie, "and you don't even know it." She pressed a blue glass bead over the hole and held it. "It's like getting to the last page of a story and then not getting to read what it says." She took her finger away.

"That looks good," Jessie said. "I hope it doesn't fall out." She touched the bead.

"Careful," Lynette told her.

"What are you girls doing out there?" Aunt Dot called.

"Just playing with our Barbies," Jessie shouted, and then she and Lynette cracked up.

Back at her own house, when Lynette came downstairs the next morning, her mother and Robert were standing at the living room window. They didn't turn around. They just stared out. Lynette doubted they'd been talking about the tulip tree's blooms or the dramatic sunrise, which her father might have pointed out was only this beautiful because the light rays had gotten tangled up in the pulp mill's polluted exhaust. No, she suspected that her mother and brother were standing there because of the window itself: that window and everything it stood for these days in this house. There was, according to Dr. Issandi, just this brief window of opportunity. Lynette was in a growth spurt, so her bones would heal well and quickly, but just for a while. They needed to strike while the iron was hot, Dr. Issandi said, which made Lynette envision a red-hot fireplace poker released and headed like an arrow toward her back.

Their mother sighed and put a hand on Robert's shoulder. "Good job on that lawn," she said. Then they turned and walked into the kitchen.

Stepping to the window, Lynette watched the garish white tulip tree blooms flutter against a mauve sky. Wet with dew, the newly cut grass shimmered, almost blue. Yesterday Robert had mowed in east-west rows across the lawn; last week he'd mowed north-south. Every night he dragged around the sprinklers. He used a push mower one week and a gas-powered one the next. She blinked into the sunrise, catching her own reflection staring back. She'd been told she'd have to wear glasses soon . . . as if having such a nose and a humped scoliotic back weren't enough.

Her mother and brother rattled dishes in the kitchen. They'd been deterred from their mission. Neither had put it that way, but Lynette could tell by the looks they gave each other— whenever it came up that Dad would be home in only three weeks—that they weren't happy about the deterrence. But it wasn't Lynette's fault. It was Great-Uncle Floyd's. He'd died.

His death set in motion a whirlwind of phone calls and baking sessions.

"It was just his time," their father had said last night to Lynette and Robert from the ship. She'd been in the kitchen, already grating carrots for a cake, the phone pressed between her left ear and shoulder, which Robert had once joked she could do so easily because her back had extra height on that side.

Robert, on the phone in their parents' bedroom, had been silent. He'd worked all day: sharpening mower blades, clipping and raking around the junipers. The lawn was a sort of pet for him, a dog he fed and groomed.

Uncle Floyd had lived a good long life, their father had said, and Lynette could almost smell the briny musk her father would soon be trailing through the house.

"See," she said, taking the phone in her left hand, "it just goes to show how you can't ever *know*. Uncle Floyd wasn't even sick. He was here, and then *zap*, he's gone."

"He had a bad heart," her mother said from across the kitchen.

Lynette turned toward her. In one ear her father was listing the many things he'd remember about Floyd: the nutty ties and his collection of pocket knives, how he loved to polka. And in her other, open ear, her mother was explaining—as if Lynette's full attention were on *her*—how Floyd had never listened to Aunt Bette, had kept on buying and cooking slab bacon even when Bette wouldn't.

Her mother had the Mixmaster on high, but suddenly she turned it off and stood frowning into the batter as if trying to remember what to put in next. Just then there was a brief lull on the phone line too, and in it Lynette thought she could hear waves breaking against the ship. Day by day, hour by hour, the *Eugenia* was settling lower into the water as the salmon landed in its hull. When one compartment filled up, a big door slammed and another opened. Her father was in charge of that: the closing and opening of those doors.

⑥

"He can't *hear* us, Mother," Lynette said when her mother told her and Robert to go say goodbye to Great-Uncle Floyd in his casket.

"Obviously I didn't mean that literally." Her mother's head jerked sharply, her nose in the center of Lynette's field of vision.

"I'm not touching him," Robert said. This was, after all, his first funeral. Patting Uncle Floyd's hands was something they'd observed several relatives do. Great-Aunt Bette stood under the window, and after someone had bid her husband goodbye, she'd take both their hands in both of hers and lift them up and down. Then Aunt Dot would pat Bette's shoulder. Her father's brothers, Mel and Carl, would shake the hands after they'd passed through Aunt Bette's. Her grandfather Ralph, Floyd's brother, sat sideways on the edge of a pew and sometimes looked up and nodded to someone who'd just completed the hand-shaking ritual. The five of them had been doing this in exactly this manner for at least twenty minutes.

While her cousin Jessie manned the lobby and the sign-in book, Lynette's mother motioned people forward to the casket.

"You two. Now." Her mother tipped her head slightly to Lynette and Robert. Her mother was nervous, Lynette knew,

17

about the desserts—eight of them—for the reception, which was to be at their house later. Her mother was not an especially good cook, and desserts ranked low on the list of what she did manage well. Lynette had never seen a homemade cheesecake come out of their oven, and this week there'd been two.

Robert pulled Lynette's arm. "Let's go," he said. "Let's do it."

But nearing the casket, they had to stop and wait behind their two distant cousins, Fran and Mary Beth, who were discussing a casserole Uncle Floyd had liked.

"That tuna one with potato chips on top?" Fran was saying. Lynette had been a flower girl in her wedding six years earlier, when Fran had been willowy and regal in the ivory dress with the gray pearl buttons. Now Fran was pudgy; even her feet seemed to jiggle over the sides of her black shoes.

"Or you can use corn flakes," Mary Beth said and smiled.

Robert hunched his shoulders and shook his head.

"Doesn't he look peaceful?" Fran asked when she finally looked into the box.

"Are you going to cry?" Robert asked Lynette when it was their turn to move ahead.

"I don't know. Maybe." They stepped forward and she stared down. The face was puffier than Uncle Floyd's. She could see powder caked in the deep creases of his cheeks.

"Who puts the makeup on?" Lynette asked Robert. Then she saw that her brother's gaze was fixed on the spray of roses over the closed bottom half of the casket.

"I'm not looking," Robert said. "I want to remember him the way he was."

"You should look," Lynette told him. "You'll be sorry later."

"I don't think so," Robert said. "I don't think I will."

At the reception Lynette brushed past Robert and her cousin Buster. She was carrying dirty cups to the kitchen and glad to be of use. "Finished with that cheesecake?" she'd ask. "How about a slice of carrot cake?" She felt serene, smug. "Decaf is no problem. I'll go make some." Today, for once, no one was saying squat about the miracle surgery. Everyone was busy at pinochle or rummy, which was, Aunt Bette said, waving her hands over the cards, just what Floyd would have wanted.

"Such a sweet girl," Fran whispered to Mary Beth as Lynette passed with the silver percolator. And "such a sweet face except for that nose" were the words Mary Beth whispered back, and which Lynette heard only because she'd stopped and turned just then in the doorway. She butted her backside hard into the door, and it swung open into the kitchen. Her face burned. They pitied her. The oversized cousins pitied *her.* Still, she was glad that for once the comments made behind her back were not about poles stuck up her spine, not about growth plates, or hip-length casts—the sorts of details her mother usually felt compelled to explain to any nosy nitwit relative.

"So I hear you want to be a professional lawn man," Uncle Mel was saying to Robert when Lynette returned with the decaf. Mel was dealing cards, and Robert—standing by the buffet table—had just taken a big bite of cake.

"He's an A-plus student in science," Aunt Dot announced to Mel and to everyone at the card table. A thin, petite woman, Dot wasn't playing, but she liked to walk up behind people and look down at their hands. She prided herself on keeping a perfect poker face.

"So he might make a doctor, then?" Aunt Mary asked, fanning out her cards. She wore rings—sometimes two or three—on almost every finger. She and Uncle Carl were divorced now, but she'd flown in from Florida, where she had a new daughter and new husband.

"So how do you feel about blood?" Uncle Mel asked Robert, and Lynette, standing behind Mel, rolled her eyes at her brother, remembering how he couldn't even look at Uncle Floyd.

"I'm not against blood," Robert said.

Yeah, right, Lynette was thinking.

An hour ago, at the cemetery, Lynette had stared into the hole, which was draped with a purple cloth as if to conceal the dirt. But clumps of damp, rust-colored earth had fallen here and there onto the cloth.

Robert had nudged her and nodded toward the digging machines that hovered like ravenous yellow dogs at the cemetery's edge.

"Backhoes," their mother whispered and then shot the equipment her own dark look. Wind whipped at the pines behind the machines. Clouds soared past each other. As the pulleys ratcheted the coffin down, her mother slipped an arm around Lynette's waist, and for a moment Lynette thought it was because she'd been standing in a too obviously slanted posture. Her mother wanted her to straighten up. Handfuls of dirt—one, then another—fell atop the polished oak box, which, it struck her, would not be shiny much longer. Then she heard her mother crying, softly. She'd been crying last night too—on the phone—and at first Lynette had thought it was about Great-Uncle Floyd. Their father was back in port now, unloading the *Eugenia*. Between sobs, Lynette had caught a few of her mother's words: . . . *my chromosomes . . . my fault.*

"Read 'em and weep," her Uncle Carl shouted now and slapped down his cards. A couple of weeks ago, he'd told Lynette he might have a job for her next summer if she'd "be a brave girl and get that back fixed up."

Lynette went into the kitchen for cream. Jessie followed her in and closed the door. She wanted to show Lynette her navel ring. Jessie pulled up her blue blouse. "It's a rattlesnake," she said about the ring. Jessie had gone, unbeknownst to Aunt Dot and Uncle Mel, to the Piercing Pagoda in the mall, where, she began explaining, a girl had used a punch machine that "barely stung for one second."

"I've had needles that stayed ten minutes in my spine," Lynette said, not taking her eyes off the silver and black snake, which was wound twice through Jessie's navel as if having gone back for a second bite.

"You don't need to say anything to your mother," Jessie said and pulled her blouse down just as the kitchen door swung open.

"Lynnie, do you know if there's any Alka-Seltzer around here?" Aunt Dot stood by the stove with her hand on her belly. "I shouldn't have eaten that cheesecake. I don't know what came over me. I'm not good with dairy."

Lynette pulled open a cupboard above the fridge. There must have been ten different kinds of stomach remedies in there. "Help yourself," she said.

Looking out the window as she ran water into a glass for Dot, she saw Grandpa Ralph in the backyard, sitting on the picnic table, playing his accordion. She cracked the window, though it was chilly outside—which was the reason, the others claimed, they were staying indoors . . . near the cakes and the cards. Her grandfather was playing songs he'd said he knew Uncle Floyd had liked. The music was sweet and slow. Lynette watched as one of his hands skimmed the ivories, while the other heaved the bellows and worked the buttons. The more air her grandfather got into the machine, the more music the machine seemed to pump back.

"I wonder who'll keep that old belly Steinway alive when he's gone," Aunt Dot asked, which was a thing Grandpa Ralph himself had often said, and which had once, years ago, made Lynette ask him in return, "Where're you going, Grandpa?" But he'd only smiled then and played some more, as he smiled now and began another song.

Her parents had stepped out for a couple of Cokes, and Robert was the only one there when Lynette came to. He wore a blue mask so only his eyes showed.

"Am I dead?" were, she was told later, the first words she said. She remembered thinking that the eyes looking down on her from the blue face were clearly Robert's, but not the same Robert. This Robert had long black eyelashes; this one reeked of something like floor polish or window cleaner.

When she woke again, her father was whistling. She recognized the tune, although it was something she suspected was no real song—just a ditty he'd made up. There were silly words . . . about waves and moonlight.

"She can have some of my Coke," she heard her brother say.

Then her mother's voice: "No, the nurse said she can only have water."

"I hate wa . . . water" was the next thing Lynette purportedly said, although she'd always have just their word for that—no actual memory of having said it.

Someone stuck a straw between her lips, which she *did* recall, as well as how her lips felt starched.

"You'll like *this* water," her mother said.

"You're fine, Lynnie," her father told her.

"The doctor said your nose took longer to fix than your back," her brother said.

"Ro-*bert*," her mother said.

Lynette blinked. She could see now that they were all wearing the blue masks, also matching blue boots and gloves, which she thought was odd but couldn't find the strength to ask about.

"Everything's fine," her father said, coming more fully into view over the white hump she suddenly realized was her bandaged nose.

Like every July, they were up at Grandpa Ralph's place on Davis Lake, just a few short miles from Canada. The ten cabins on his road—all but his—had names: Harmony Hut, Taking a Break, Sunny Dawn. Grandpa Ralph's had a mailbox with a huge wooden fish, its scales made of tin can lids, hanging over it.

It was the Fourth, and her two uncles and her father were sitting on the couch watching a news reporter ask Buzz Aldrin and Neil Armstrong if they felt ready for the trip next week to the moon. The astronauts beamed into the cabin's crowded living room. They couldn't wait, they said.

"Walking on the moon! Did you think we'd ever see such a thing?" her Grandpa Ralph piped up from the armchair.

The three men nodded solemnly, their shoulders touching, the three identical suntanned necks below the light brown hair.

In the kitchen Lynette's mother and Aunt Dot were canning cucumbers while Lynette set the table. She felt like some sort of capsule herself, drifting between the male planet of cosmic occurrences and the female one of steam and vinegar and jars that would later, in the middle of dinner, make tiny little popping sounds as their lids sealed.

Buster followed Lynette around the table, picking up the forks and knives and shining them with a dishtowel. He wouldn't speak to her unless she stood right in front of him and put her face close to his, which Uncle Carl had recently explained to her was the best way. "Thanks, Buster," she said now, "you're doing a good job."

"Are we having pickles for dinner?" he asked.

It was a reasonable question. Lynette tried to peer deeper into those sky-blue eyes of his that just blinked and blinked. "No, salmon. We always have salmon on the Fourth."

He was in her brother Robert's class, and once she'd heard him tell Uncle Carl that "tucking in shirttails was not something 'the normals' did," meaning, she supposed, Robert and his little-league pals.

After Uncle Mel had teased her about the gold ring in her nose—saying her cave people friends were looking for her—she'd stormed out, slamming the back door.

This was the first time today that Lynette had been allowed to stand up and walk around. She'd spent most of the last week lying down, on a blanket in the grass. Her torso felt like a set of three perfectly aligned logs—two metal ones and a bone one—that someone could come by and roll into the lake.

Her father had just put a whole salmon—after covering it with the rind of a lime Lynette had grated—inside the domed grill out back. He knew a hundred recipes. Salmon was brain food, he told them. At home they had a freezer full of it. "We'll all be much smarter soon," her mother would say each time she opened the freezer door.

After their meal, Lynette was excused from the cleanup. Grandpa Ralph played his accordion out on the dock as the sun went down, and Lynette called to him from her blanket, saying maybe when she was better, she might want to try playing that thing, and he nodded, thinking this over. Then he mentioned he'd heard of a woman down in Reno who could play with the best of them.

Now her father gave a long, high whistle as the first firecracker went off across the lake. It was never a big show or a long one because the Davis Lake Homeowners' Association was small and cheap and of the collective mind that kids should be in bed by ten.

Besides the nose "fix," Lynette had agreed to the surgery on one other condition: her list of what would and wouldn't be acceptable if she *didn't* pull through. It had one word at the top: *if.* Two weeks ago she'd laid the list at the center of the kitchen table next to a platter of salmon in hot peanut sauce, her favorite of her father's concoctions. She'd drawn blanks at the bottom of the page for everyone's signature. Items on the list: *No casket, cremation a must, no viewing of the body by anyone before it is burnt. Ashes to be scattered across Davis Lake at dusk as the song (#3 cut, "Fields of Time" from the Fat Nothing tape) plays. Absolutely no speeches.* She'd passed around pens and watched while each person signed. Then she'd made them Swear To God.

"Water my feet," she said to Robert now, and he squirted them with a mister. She couldn't bend to put on socks or tie her shoes. People had to help her do these simple things. And for some reason her toes itched. Her father teased that it was just the mosquitoes.

She had not had to go to camp last week, a place where mosquitoes ruled. She had not had to endure the cold baths in the creek, or the sing-alongs, the lame talent night, or the lamer-still lanyard hour.

Jessie and Buster sat on the dock dangling their feet in the water. Her father whistled again. A rocket had blown open, and out of it drizzled streamers of green, blue, and gold. Buster covered his ears. She wished some of the drizzle would fall—still blazing—into the lake, but that never happened. To see the fireworks, she had to turn her head, an undertaking accompanied by small jolts of pain, but ones she was getting used to. She felt like a giant moth larva that was still weeks away from busting headfirst out of its white pupal sheath.

She had a very small gold hoop in her new left nostril, which made her mother wince each time she looked closely at Lynette. Her mother was, she'd said, "a little hurt and a little insulted" about the nose. It no longer resembled her own. And lately, looking in the mirror, Lynette could already feel the exact sadness she knew she'd feel from now on whenever she stared at the nose, although she liked it and was, in general, pleased with the newness of her face. Still, there was a prick of regret as she smiled into her own smile.

"It looks like a gold booger's trying to get out of your nose," Robert whispered to her, but she just watched the sky. Soon, very soon, two men would be stepping on that moon. Hand in hand, her mother and father walked down to the rocky beach. They'd be like this for a couple more weeks, since her father was still, as he said, "reacclimating to land." It was what he always said for the first few weeks he was home.

From across the lake came "The 1812 Overture" on someone's tape player, and Grandpa Ralph waved his hands in the air as if directing the orchestra.

Three silver rockets shot up—bam, bam, bam—then opened and dripped down.

"Ooo," everyone said as the silver sparks cascaded and descended and disappeared at the glass surface of the lake.

When at last the music stopped, all the frogs and crickets started up as if on cue. The Fourth of July had been a long time coming, and the frogs were late this year, still busy at what Grandpa Ralph called their mating songs. Lynette closed her eyes. Beneath her the ground felt warmer, and above, the air seemed cooler. She felt herself—the longer, sleeker length of her—a conduit through which the weather was shifting. Meanwhile the crickets, sensing they had the airwaves to themselves now, cranked up the volume—as if they couldn't believe it was finally summer and they were here, alive, as if they had to sing like that to be sure.

⑥

The Ides

The wind kept blowing the ashes back landward. Knee-deep in the ocean, Jessie's mother turned away from the beach and shook the urn harder. The wind was blowing the wrong way. That was the problem.

"I'm going out farther," she said. "You girls stay here." But Abby, as always, ignored their mother and waded out too. The white froth of the surf was past her chubby little knees.

Jessie obeyed. She even took a step back, onto the damp sand, not the stinging swirling sand. She was carrying the blankets to dry everyone's feet when they'd finished. Including her own pair, she had three pairs of socks in her pockets—since she, apparently, was the only one with pockets.

The waves rolled across her mother's thighs. She'd been crying for weeks. But finally she wasn't. She was serious, watching the ash lift on the breeze. She kept brushing specks of it off her cheeks. She'd been crying because she'd wanted to stand—as she was right now—on the Kona coast her husband had loved. She'd been waiting for Jessie's spring break. She didn't want Jessie to get behind in school. God forbid she would have to repeat the third grade. March 15. They could go then.

Jessie watched a plume of ash drift away over her mother's head, and she imagined some bit of her father's bone as a speck of grit in a seagull's eye. The gulls were everywhere. Her father was with the gulls. That was the thought going through her mind when the rest happened.

Jessie heard the splash and saw Abby look up and laugh. She'd tripped somehow. Suddenly she was fully in the water, sitting in it. Then a wave hit her, tumbled her over, and their mother was moving toward her. Her mother's two long white arms went down in the water, and Jessie watched as the lacey white edges of the wave enveloped those arms and then the rest of her mother.

Jessie still had the blankets. She held them above her head as she ran toward the water. "Mom!" she called. She stood waist-deep where her mother, no more than a minute ago, had entered the water.

"I've got her!" her mother shouted. She had surfaced about thirty feet out. Her face flashed at the top of a wave.

Jessie craned her neck, squinting to see. She thought she saw Abby's curly red hair. Then she saw her mother's legs. They were kicking frantically. But her mother seemed to be swimming parallel to the beach, not *toward* it.

Jessie took another couple of steps into the surf, then pivoted and threw the blankets as far and hard as she could behind her.

When she turned back, she couldn't see her mother's legs anymore. The surf banged against her own legs like cold boulders. How could her father have loved this sea? He'd surfed here as a boy, and after he was killed in Vietnam's Ia Drang Valley, her mother had a duty, she'd said, to carry out his wishes.

"Mom," Jessie called again, but she could barely hear her own voice. There wasn't anyone out there: no boats, no swimmers, no kids on surfboards.

Jessie glanced back toward the blankets. They'd landed on the damp sand, and she knew that her mother would be furious when she and Abby swam back in and found the blankets all wet and gritty.

Her mother's feet. Those firm pink toes. That was the last Jessie had seen of her.

Two days later, her sister's body had washed ashore thirty-seven miles south of Kona, which made it about seventy miles, her Uncle Mel said, from the beach where they'd spread the ashes. Everyone had talked about a current. They said the deep currents had yanked Abby and Jessie's mother right off the island's edge. The natives had stories of similar disappearances going back hundreds of years.

Jessie's mother, Helen Marie Clarkson, had not been found. Jessie was eight when this happened, and for over a year she pinned a great many hopes on the dolphins. She felt sure there was a sea cove somewhere on the island that no one had searched yet. She refused to believe what she'd overheard Aunt Dot, her mother's sister, tell Lynette's mother on the phone: "They're saying all hope is lost now. Oh, Cheryl, I *try* not to let her see me cry."

And who was this "they"? Jessie wondered. How could such a thing be known for sure?

Jessie had heard so many stories. Back there on the beach. From the teenagers who'd found her. Those dolphins. Evidently they often helped out tired swimmers, giving them a lift to shore. Jessie's dreams were full of dolphins splashing, spraying water in her face. They leapt out from the depths of sea caves, frolicked through the lava-warmed waters. They had huge smiling mouths.

Jessie refused to weep the huge, body-shaking sobs Aunt Dot cried. She kept an image of her mother's reemergence in her mind, and later, for years, a feeling, an opening in her heart. She could picture the cove. The dolphins were a family there, and just as Dot and Mel had taken Jessie in, so had the dolphins taken in her mother to live with them. Her mother swam like a mermaid now. She ate raw fish and picked bananas from a tree.

At her new school in Spokane, Jessie, and only Jessie, was allowed to call Mrs. Lundstrum, the school psychologist, Aunt Cheryl. Aunt Cheryl asked Jessie if she'd like to draw her dream. Jessie was terrible at drawing, but the idea began to seem more appealing when Aunt Cheryl Lundstrum opened her drawer and took out the box of brand-new colored pencils—not crayons!—and a large sheet of thick beige paper. Jessie sat in a sunlit foyer of the library. She began with that banana tree. In the opened box, the pencils were lined up like soldiers. Soldiers awaiting the most daunting duties. Jessie reached for the gray one. Out of all the colors—so newly sharpened and glistening—she knew she must begin with the dull gray pencil. No question. She slipped it from the box. Gray was the color of the water that day. Gray was the color of the dolphins too. She touched the gray pencil tip to the paper. For real, she was saying to herself. There was a wave, she whispered. It could be bluer, she thought. It could go higher. Water seemed impossible to draw. There'd been white and yellow inside it . . . possibly a turquoise hue where the wave had curled into itself.

Jessie could not recall the sky. Not the beach. Not even the urn, which she vaguely remembered had washed up near her feet by the surf as she'd stood there waiting. For how many minutes? Hours? Then she'd gotten cold and bundled up in the damp blankets and sat on the dry, prickly sand until those teenagers had come to smoke dope there at sunset and found her and wouldn't believe what she said had happened. She kept showing them the urn.

——

Her new cousin Lynette had given Jessie her old pink bicycle and ridden in front of her on a bigger yellow bike, showing Jessie where to make one left turn and then another, and then how to ride up over the curb onto the long, winding, tree-shaded street that would get her to her new school. Then Lynette made Jessie go in front and show that she knew the way.

At school the coloring wasn't going well. Those afternoons with the colored pencils. Jessie kept wanting to work on the same drawing, but Aunt Cheryl wanted her to try another one, something new. "What about that banana tree?" her aunt asked. Aunt Cheryl was kind. She smiled. She just shrugged if Jessie said no, no thanks. This aunt wore earrings that matched a ring on her finger: black opals, she told Jessie. Jessie recalled a particular peach-colored pencil her aunt had held out to her. She'd watched her own fingers move toward it. For real, she told herself, yes, there might have been just a tiny speck of this peach color in the big wave she was working on. But then she'd felt less certain. No, maybe she only wanted there to be. She was trying, she told Aunt Cheryl. She was trying to get it right.

She asked for another sheet of paper—not to start again, but to attach the new sheet to the left side of the drawing in progress. She needed to extend the shore southward, to convey the overwhelmingness of the water. Jessie added more black lines. Pulses were what she told Aunt Cheryl these were. Underneath the pulses were the dolphins, happily wriggling and gliding and executing all manner of rolls and spins and flips, but only these pulses—here and here and here—were visible to the naked eye.

One-Eyed with Patrice and the Gnomes

Lynette, age 40, 1997

Yesterday, in a lawn chair at the Willow Motel, an eight-year-old named Patrice read to me. A ridiculous story with gnomes and rocketing rocking chairs. But she read it well, never stumbling over any of the words that to me resembled pebbles in sand.

A semi-blind woman is likely to believe in gnomes; therefore, Patrice feels it's important to point out that they're not real. Just made-up, she interjects every three or four pages as she reads the book again. If something bad happens, she tells me, don't think it's for real.

When the last gnome has blasted into space, Patrice leads me across the parking lot. Her family has a little cat-sized dog they call Boo. Boo! they shout when they put their heads out the door—a cry that unnerves me five doors down at noon in my dark number 17.

Her father, driving them here in a sleek silver minivan, came to get his eyes fixed. He'll go back to the clinic and get his new vision inspected, and they'll be gone tomorrow. I'd said I'd watch the girl, although "watch" may be overstating it.

I stay and stay. Still here. Still unhealed. I was supposed to remain under wraps—in the room, in the dark. But I need some air today, I told the orderly, and yes, I'll keep the patch on, and don't worry, I'll tell any patients I see that I'm an anomaly and I'm on the mend.

Bad Boo, Patrice scolds when the dog licks my ankles. She walks me to the edge of the highway. She is the eye of the day. This is the road to the United States, she says. But don't go out there, Lynette. She pulls me to the other side of the parking lot and points out a movie theater, the high school, and the mall, which she says is a joke. All of that's on the other side of the black roiling river.

I remember something I liked from a college class: in Chinese poetry, a river's mist distorts vision. This is to remind us that in a realm of words, we reside behind a seer's eyes, and that the seer is mortal—and thus imperfect.

The orderly gets out of the van with Patrice's parents. I recognize the white pants and coat. Dad, Patrice calls, can you see me? He turns. He's not even bandaged. Wow, he shouts, since when did you get so big? Boo! the mother shouts. A brown shadow stops at the side of the road. The shrill whine of compression brakes squeals around us. Boo, Boo, get back here.

Funeral of the Virgin

Lynette, age 39, 1996

It was the dress Lynette recognized first in that film. Not the face. Her *own* face. Her grandmother and mother had been married in that dress, her Aunt Dot, and two distant cousins, Fran and Mary Beth. Lynette had worn it last. Ten years ago. And maybe one day her cousin Jessie would wear it. The dress had gray-black pearls sewn into the bodice. Not white ones, which at the reception her husband Jack had said he thought was "weird," but which she promptly explained were "all people could get during the war."

"That's right," her Great-Aunt Bette chimed in, since she'd been the one to tell Lynette that in the first place.

Jack had smiled and made a toast to the dress. A haunting gesture when she recalls it now. By then they'd been sipping the pricey champagne from plastic glasses—fluted to look real—for a couple hours.

Lynette adored the dress. When she spun in it, the ivory skirt billowed like a sail. Also, the bodice gave her cleavage, something she'd never had before. Her cousin Jessie's push-up bra and some handfuls of tissue had helped. In the hotel, as she hung the dress in its garment bag, she felt a splinter of sadness prick her happiness, knowing she'd never see it again.

Except she had. That she happened to be *in* the dress when she saw it again seemed somehow less significant.

6

It was only by chance that she'd walked past the dorm's lounge where the film was playing, glanced in, and recognized the dress, and then herself. With her hair pinned up and a few trellises of curls trailing down over each temple, she was clearly the bride waving from atop the backseat of someone's convertible. The tiny hoop she'd worn in her nose since she was twelve glinted in the sun. She had on the ivory gloves she'd bought at Goodwill, the ones with gray faux pearl buttons. And yes, she thought: that too was right. It had all happened exactly like this—but ten years ago, years that seemed now from another life, from someone *else's* life.

She stood in the lounge doorway watching, her thoughts stalled on the one thing that *didn't* seem right. In real life, Jack had been up there beside her on the car. He'd also been waving. Also smiling. He'd worn a gray tux, although with his blond hair and fair skin, gray was not a good color for him. It washed him out. Who cares? he'd said. He would wear gray if she wanted him to, and she did; she'd been determined to match Jack with those pearls from the war. This struck her now: her former fervency, her zeal. And Jack, dear Jack—whatever she asked, he'd do. No sacrifice seemed too great for her greater happiness.

Still, seeing the dress again and herself in it, she was surprised there was no Jack. She pushed her glasses higher on her nose, squinting, as if a more accurate focus would bring him into view. In the film the convertible was turning up Monroe Street. Yes, that had been the route.

She stepped into the room, a basement lounge in Hadley Hall. She'd been on her way to do laundry in the room next door.

"What is this?" she asked the boy who was watching the film. "What *is* this show?"

"I have no idea," he said. "Something for my film class."

Lynette stared at the TV screen. From *her*, the bride atop the car, the film cut back and forth to images of men in hardhats working at terrifying heights on skyscrapers. Men and cranes. Grainy cityscapes.

"So it's a tape, then? A movie?"

"Yeah," the boy said. "Just one of many pieces of shit I've had to endure ad nauseam this weekend. I'm trying to catch up. I've been sick."

From every direction, Lynette felt questions press in, and a surge of anger too, which she couldn't quite account for but knew she wanted to direct toward the boy—until, that is, he mentioned he'd been sick. Now she had to reconsider the accusatory tone in which her questions sat poised. Oh, she thought, he's been sick.

She set her basket of laundry on the floor. Okay, she told herself, the boy's just catching up on his class. She was, after all, in his dorm, and although it was a co-ed residence, she wasn't a student—in fact had never been a student—at this college. Hadley Hall's laundry facilities were simply convenient for her, only three blocks from the little house she rented.

She sat down on the heap of dirty clothes in her basket and watched her younger self wave to her older self, and to the boy who'd begun popping pretzels into his mouth. The videotape footage was black-and-white. Huge sledgehammers rose and fell on steel beams. The boy had the sound turned low. The clanging *was* annoying, and she could hardly blame him.

"What's the name of this?" she asked.

He lifted the tape slipcase. "Funeral of the Virgin," he read off its side.

"Never heard of it."

"No one has. No one's heard of anything we see for this class."

"May I look at that?" She nodded to the case.

The boy sighed. He had to lift his red-socked feet off the chair in front of him to lean over and pass her the case. "What time is it?" he asked as he did. "It's not morning yet, is it?" He rubbed his eyes.

"Yep," she said, "but just barely." She rarely ran into students in the dorm basement. She liked to do her laundry early, before the students were up, before they could possibly rouse themselves after raucous all-night parties, audible three blocks away when she cracked her window.

"Morning," the boy said and yawned. She wasn't sure if he'd offered a greeting or the acknowledgment of a fact.

In the room's dim light, Lynette bent close to the case to read what little there was on the back. *Produced and directed by T. Emory Lazarre, 1988.* The film had been made eight years ago—two years *after* her wedding.

She looked up. The footage showed a close-up of her face. She'd had less of a double chin then, and a smile that seemed to suggest some gay abandon. The Lynette of the film was without her glasses, and she remembered now how she'd had to be led around by the hand that day, first by her bridesmaid, Jessie, and then by her husband, Jack. Only after the dress had been stowed in the closet and she had her glasses back on had she turned and seen herself in the hotel mirror: a wife then, a Mrs.

"Who's T. Emory Lazarre?" she asked the boy. "I hope I'm not bothering you."

"He's the shithead teacher. We have to watch three of his films. They're all lame like this one." He sighed again and glanced around at Lynette. "My paper's due at one o'clock. To*day*."

Lynette nodded. A student's life was hard. She remembered that. She'd gone to a small private college across town. There were many demands. Someone could pop a quiz without the slightest provocation, like a big hatchet falling across the most pleasant of mornings.

"What have you got so far?" she asked him.

He read her a single sentence: *The plain-faced young bride is on her way to her wedding, which is meant to symbolize her death, i.e., the end of her carefree adolescence.* He rolled his eyes. "That's it," he said.

"Sounds good," Lynette told him, although she was thinking how the bride had actually already been to her wedding and was on her way instead to a reception at the Highland Fairways Club House. It had been, she recalled, a very hot day, and those moments riding on the car's backseat had been the day's only cool ones.

She and the boy watched as the camera panned: skyscrapers and mist circled a lake. Lynette leaned forward. No, that couldn't be her town. Her town didn't have a lake.

"*Finally* the end," the boy said when the screen flickered and went black.

"Maybe," she offered—"maybe that girl represents some virgin who's been sacrificed to the gods?" Lynette had been a literature major herself, and she could still recall a thing or two about symbolism.

"The gods?" the boy asked.

"You know, like the gods of capitalism."

The TV sputtered a loud static. "What?" The boy sat up straighter. "Can you repeat that? What you just said."

She said it again.

His dark brown eyes focused on her mouth. "That's *it*, I bet. Mind if I use that?" He smiled then, his eyes widening in an innocent questioning look, which made Lynette guess that he was the kind of boy who'd think nothing of writing math equations on his palms before an exam.

"Sure," she said, lifting her hand. "It's yours."

"So it's kind of like the end of our country's innocence too?" he asked.

His question startled her. She'd been assuming he was a bit of a dolt. But now, now she understood that he must have just been tired. He'd been sick. He hadn't been able to concentrate well.

"Urban industrialization," she said, watching him write.

"Yeah," he said, "the world's on fire"—he was writing and talking at the same time—"and this girl's getting pitched to the flames. Bye-bye, purity."

"You're not bad at this," Lynette said. "I bet you'll get an A."

His pen flew to the next line of his yellow legal pad. "Good," he said, "I need to. I've only got a C minus so far. It's just good bullshit teachers are after, isn't it? Maybe I'm finally getting the knack."

"Yes," she said, "I think you are."

He nodded and stared at the notepad. "I wish it hadn't taken me five semesters."

The next day Lynette watched the film while she grated cheese and whipped eggs. After work, she'd gone to the college library and checked it out at the reserve desk, just as the boy in Hadley Hall had told her she could. She'd used her community resident ID card, which also admitted her to the school gym and the big blue pool. When the student library worker had asked whether she was enrolled in the film class, since only film students could check out the tapes, Lynette had lied—way too easily, she thought later. "I'm auditing," she'd said, and the young woman had scowled, shrugged, and handed over the tape.

Lynette rewound it and watched it again while she chopped leeks, then once more while she sewed a button on the turquoise blouse she'd gotten at Nu-2-Yu, a secondhand store on Sprague Avenue. The film was truly dreadful, though mercifully, it was short. No semblance of story—not even a snippet of the pre-wedding romance, not a smidgen of courtship. It was all jump cut and slow zoom. She wasn't a hundred percent sure of the film lingo.

She debated about whether or not she'd show it to Rory, her boyfriend, but when he appeared at six, bearing a loaf of focaccia bread and a bottle of good pinot noir, she ran the film a fourth time.

The leek tart was baking—quite aromatically—in the oven. "I just want you to see something," she said to him.

Rory, on the couch, was removing his shoes. It was tax season, and he'd been cranking out decimal points all day at his firm. "My god," he said and stood up, dangling one brown wingtip by its laces. He stepped toward the TV. "That *girl.* That bride-girl." He put his face close to the screen. "Is that you, Lynette?"

"It's me all right."

"Where's Jack?" was what Rory said next. "Where's your husband?"

Rory's question, she thought, was a good one. No Jack. No Jack anywhere to be seen. As she swam laps, Lynette reheard the answers she'd given to Rory, as well as a few she *hadn't* given. The answers had a soggy underwater feel.

It seemed a rather odd coincidence to her (if *odd* was even the word) that her husband, who was now absent from her life, was also absent from the film. Maybe this was more an irony than a coincidence, or were ironies always coincidences? Possibly just the good ones?

She came to the end of the pool, turned, and started back across. She'd lost count of what lap she was on.

After a fifth rerunning of the film, Rory had come to this determination: she should waste no time; she should sue Mr. T. Emory Whomever. That man couldn't just use her face that way. He couldn't appropriate those very private moments from her life.

"You know what litigation is?" she'd asked him, remembering one of her boss's jokes from the previous week.

Rory had given her a stern look. He wasn't in the mood.

"A machine which you go into as a horse and come out of as dog food."

"Still," Rory had said, "we ought to talk to a lawyer. We should get in this Emory person's face."

At the shop where she worked, the Chef's Pal, older stock—packages of lentil soup mix and huckleberry teas—had been removed. New stock would go in those places as soon as

Lynette wiped the shelves clean. The Chef's Pal sold seven sizes of whisks; one aisle was devoted to garlic accouterments: presses and peelers, roasters and keepers. Eighty-eight cookie cutters—in copper and stainless steel—eagles, donkeys, ballerinas, lighthouses, cowboys—hung on a wall, and it was Lynette's job to keep them shiny.

Mr. Kinney, her boss, offered jokes—a new one every day—to the customers while they shopped. *You know what the group of traveling ladies said to their airplane pilot? Now, don't go flying faster than sound—we want to talk.*

He found the jokes, Lynette was sure, in some joke book from the fifties. The jokes were as clean as the shelves. She imagined him going through the book with Stan, the man he called his "very dear friend," and picking out a Tuesday joke, a Wednesday joke. He'd give a little hiccup-like chortle after the punch line.

Know what a mummy is? An Egyptian that was pressed for time.

As Mr. Kinney repeated today's joke for the umpteenth time, Lynette closed her eyes and saw her dress again—its pearl buttons shimmering, even in the grainy film. Now her whole wedding had blurred into that footage. The ceremony seemed to have taken place atop a skyscraper. The groom, apparently, had slipped off a beam.

It's only been in the last couple years that she has quit missing Jack in the achingly numbing way she missed him just after he was gone. But now, all over again—as if it's happened only today, eight years later, with her on a stepladder—the old shock of loss digs in, familiar, as recognizable as that dress.

Thirty-six shelves are spic-and-span, and Mr. Kinney's chuckles about mummies have a dreary, lifeless feel. He can't see what Lynette sees: how the customers roll their eyes. By closing time, he'll have no clue that he's become a stutter of the day's refrain. Yes, yes, they were—we are all—pressed for time.

⑥

On Professor Lazarre's head, just above his small wire-rimmed glasses, was a shiny bald spot. Lynette couldn't stop staring at it. His hair, fluffed out around the spot, was the color of rusted iron.

Professor Lazarre had launched into elaborate detail about each of his three films. No doubt he assumed that was why she'd come. First there'd been one called *No Time Outs,* which was inspired, he said, by the life of a young football teammate who'd sustained a crippling injury. The second film, *Torch-Bearer,* had received X, Y, and Z awards, awards she'd never heard of. But yes, the one she was asking about, *Funeral of the Virgin,* was, he felt sure, his best. In fact, he added, the best student paper he'd seen on that film had come in just yesterday— and from one of his worst students ever. A sad case, really, he told her. The student was a boy whose leukemia had taken an unexpected turn for the worse.

Lynette took a breath and let it out slowly. The office suddenly felt hot and close. She wanted to sit down, but Lazarre was sitting in his desk chair, and the only other chair was piled high with papers. The boy from Hadley Hall and his bright red socks flashed before her eyes.

"That footage of the bride—"

"Oh yes," he interrupted her, "I believe I may have gotten that years ago when I worked at Walgreens. I was putting myself through school. Working in the camera department. I made copies of wedding videos for couples to give away. The technology was so new then. It was a store on Northwest Boulevard . . ." He rambled on.

By then it had become excruciatingly clear to her that he did not find her, the Lynette who stood before him in her turquoise blouse, even remotely recognizable.

"That bride was *me*," she said. "I'm not happy about being in your film."

He frowned at her, then offered a faint smile. "I don't think that's you," he said. "I rather doubt it."

"Possibly some laws have been broken, Professor Lazarre." Her questions and accusations had queued up in a long line, each one impatient.

He blinked and shook his head. He seemed to be trying to remember, to think back harder, further. That *was*, after all, what he'd made her do. And not so much a recollection of the wedding itself or of the sweet months preceding it when she and Jack had camped in the Ozarks and kayaked in Kentucky and come home in a rush to pass final exams and try on tuxes and veils and silvery patent-leather shoes. No, not those days so much as the days—a flat, almost interminable stretch of them—two years into their marriage, days abruptly devoid of Jack, of Jack's voice, his touch, his truck horn in the drive, days she had just begun to believe were, at last, dimming in her memory.

"My husband wasn't *in* the film," Lynette said flatly, feeling her eyes well up. "Jack," she said. "His name was Jack. So you just cut him out? Is that what you did?"

Lazarre sat down in his desk chair, his eyes riveted to her face. She sensed she had somehow gained an inscrutable authority over the cramped room with its jumble of books and files, though there was a window with a view of the Selkirk

Mountains, which were, just then, a lovely blue and ringed by clouds.

"I'm not remembering well," Lazarre said. "There *was* a groom, of course."

"A blond man."

"Yes, I believe that's correct."

A tear from her right eye, then one from her left, dripped ridiculously down her cheeks. And at that particular moment, she couldn't be bothered to wipe them away. Tears. These too were remnants, vestiges.

Professor Lazarre folded and refolded his hands, recrossed his legs. "I worked in such a damn hurry back then," he said. "There'd be spliced bits of film lying about, or maybe I made too many copies of something by mistake, and I had so many projects due . . . am I making sense? Is any of this clear?"

No. No, she would not bring suit. "Rory," she'd said, "that teacher is one of God's most profoundly asinine creatures." In her mind his bald spot glared like a beacon. The tiny glasses accentuated his eyes' beadiness, which in turn heightened all that was insidious about Professor Lazarre.

"Just get over it now," she said to Rory. "That's what I'm doing."

"He needs to be taken down a peg," Rory tried again. Rory had that strength and a dogged determination she would admire for another few months, and then . . . not.

"That'd be like trying to get blood from a, a . . ." She couldn't remember how that went.

"*Corpse?*" Rory shrugged. "*Turnip?*"

"He's broke," Lynette said. "His shoes have holes in the soles. How often do you see that in this day and age? Besides, I don't think there is any lower peg."

Later, in her bed, she and Rory lay curled together. She'd grown to like the way his knees pressed into the backs of her knees, how warm his thighs were against her cool ones. It'd taken almost a year to get used to this new body beside her. And recently Rory had been holding her a little longer each night, and more closely. He'd witnessed a few teary episodes himself, which she did not entirely regret.

During one, she'd told him about the two men who'd come knocking on her door eight years ago—two years after the honeymoon she and Jack had taken to Vegas, and after they'd quit their jobs at the horrid disco place, Retro Blast, where they'd met when he was a dishwasher and she danced in a skimpy black outfit she'd prefer to forget, to leave back there in what used to be the murkier, distant past.

One of the men at the door was a policeman. The other wore a brown suit with every button buttoned. When she first looked out the peephole and saw the suited man, she thought they must be selling vacuums or encyclopedias. A sad way, she thought, to make a living. Then she saw the policeman. She recognized that uniform.

Behind her the TV was on, its same sad news on all three channels: the *Challenger,* first its white exhaust zigging and zagging, and then over and over it explodes. In slow motion. What-Went-Wrong continues to be the subject of debate. The voices guess; they theorize, assume, and agree, as meanwhile, the explosion recurs.

Lynette opened the door.

Jack was still at work. He was obviously running late, and as she let the two men in, she was wishing he would honk and drive up into their driveway in his little black pickup.

The man in the suit said he was from the Burlington Northern Railroad. Hadn't he handed her a card? The policeman had definitely shown her his badge—just before he'd said something about an accident. The black pickup hadn't been crossing at a regular crossing site, the railway man told her; it was an access road—for train equipment only. Might she know why he'd been out there? On that particular road? So far from the city?

Suddenly the man in the suit walked over and turned off the TV. Lynette had almost forgotten that: how for a moment the rocket's explosions had been the only sound in the room, and then the man pushed a button and the set went black.

Neither man had even said *dead* yet when they asked her those questions, and she hadn't yet asked. The men were sitting in the new matching plaid chairs and she on the old lumpy couch. She had been trying to answer their questions, to *think* of the answers—which suddenly struck her, as she told Rory the story, as crazy, completely addle-headed.

Maybe he was taking a shortcut, she'd proposed to the two men. Maybe the load of computer tables he'd been hauling to the warehouse where he worked—maybe that heavy load had weighed his truck down and he'd gotten stuck on those tracks.

Had she really told the men this, or had she only wondered these things later, after they'd left? Now she wasn't sure. Maybe the men had told *her* they surmised he'd gotten stuck out there. At any rate, that was what was finally decided. That was the explanation everyone agreed on. They had, all three of them, nodded. And when she remembered it now, she could recall how the men had glanced at one another as they nodded. This was a new but very real part of the memory: how their glance had said okay, then, that truck must have stalled.

She'd certainly always remembered, and quite clearly, how she'd asked the men if she'd have to go somewhere to identify the body. As she told Rory this part, she thought possibly it was something she'd seen in movies and felt, somehow, would be required of her. She was terrified that it would.

The men had looked down at their hands. "No," the policeman said after a moment. No, he didn't think that would be necessary.

But it wasn't until a few hours after the service, and after she'd shared the ashes from the urn with Jack's parents, that she'd realized—completely and inescapably—*why* she hadn't had to go. Because there'd been too little of a body left to identify.

She'd understood this when she opened the small white box a man from the funeral home had handed her. Inside was Jack's wedding ring—bent, crushed, no longer identifiable as ever having been a circle.

In the pool she swam harder, longer, faster. She told herself that when she reached this next side, or maybe the next, she'd have better answers, or there'd be fewer questions. She'd stop wondering about the new idea that had never crossed her mind before, but which was now, through these last few days, in constant crossing: what *had* Jack been doing out there on that road?

She pulled back fistfuls of water. *What, what, what?* She kicked and breathed, breathed and kicked.

If a person *had* wanted to die, had wanted to end his life in a way that'd mean no further questions and a goodly sum of insurance money for the left-behind spouse—if a person had wanted to go, to be thoroughly gone, then *that* way, she kept thinking, that way was a good one. Jack would be—he had been—smart enough to think of it.

Considering this now made her replay minuscule memories from the two short years of her marriage. She tried to see these bits in a starker light, or in slow motion and a black-and-white grittiness. Every argument. Were there many? What constituted a usual number? Had he slept too often too far over on his side of the bed?

The pool water seemed to thicken with questions, a blue sludge of them, each new and developing one complicating an earlier one. And circling all of them was that huge overriding question, which seemed to take up too much space in her lane. She flung her arms. She had to carve a path through everything. She saw a plaid chair with Jack in it. Hadn't he disliked those new friends of hers, Eddie and Marlene, who had the little sick pet—what *was* it? Yes, some sort of tiny pig. And hadn't her new short haircut set him off one night? Wasn't there a tiff over mauve lipstick?—undeniably, a bad shade for her.

There were disagreements, yes, but too many? Or maybe he'd been unhappy at work? Maybe he was overworked? Exhausted? Had there been some clinical depression she should have recognized but didn't? Or had his pickup truly and simply just stalled out? A *real* accident? Not one invented in her living room by two men and a stunned young woman.

Also in the pool was the cold and heavy train itself. A black streak through the dense blue water. When it roared past her, there was an engineer waving from a small square window. He tipped his cap. More laps. She kicked and breathed. His face grew familiar, his wave cheerier. She felt sorry for him. She knew what he hadn't seen yet, what was waiting up ahead on that track.

The Crew

Robert, age 17, 1973

It takes half a Saturday afternoon for my sister, two cousins, and me to white-out the cigarette ad on the billboard. Our white brushes glide over two old dames whose arched smiles emit blue menthol. Jessie works on the black eyebrows. She's the youngest but the fastest of the four of us. Buster and I eradicate the six-foot-tall red cigarette pack that's already had a couple coats, but still a little pink shows through. To someone who didn't know better, it might seem that my sister Lynette likes what she's doing: obliterating the sky.

The Pampas Room. Oat Salve. Six-Salts. The once-was we transform into the never-been. Rescinding promises, old beckonings. *So what,* we say to Buster when he tells us the number of diamonds in the smoking lady's bracelet. It's almost May, but another light snow has started; already it's filling up the little ruptured gulleys in the dirt down below.

"Robert, look. Here he comes," Jessie says and points as our boss, Mr. Wendell Hardwick, drives off the highway's shoulder, rolls down his window, and flashes a wave toward the scaffold. Then, as usual, he just sits in his car with the dome light on. Reading a newspaper. Often, a patrol car slows and pulls over, and then Mr. Wendell Hardwick will get out and help the patrolman heft a crate of some birds—pheasants, I think—out of the trooper's trunk and into Mr. Hardwick's. The men are usually laughing as they do this. The birds are still alive, and as they're transferred between trunks, they send out shrill shrieks, like very old people being lashed with whips. It's a difficult sound to hear. Most of the time the four of us can't help ourselves; we stop the brushes and stare. But not today. We are tired today. We have miles to go, more to do, to eliminate, more to be done with.

X'd-out days. Bright dawns with us up here and the sun whiting-out the road behind us. From our scaffold we're supposed to see nothing but billboard. Not the silver cigar cutter or the silver flask on the trooper's front seat. Never those crates. We might pause and watch a train's diesel engine huff toward us, then past us. It pulls containers of cattle, coal, sawdust. However white we are up here in our painter's pants, the dust from the dust cars marks us. White minds, white air. The scaffold sways.

Later, across a greasy table at Von's diner, Mr. Wendell Hardwick's gold-ringed fingers pass us new radio batteries and white envelopes of five- and ten-dollar bills. He always asks my cousin Buster how he and his dad are doing all on their own, and Buster always stares down at his fries and says, *Good*. I think our boss is a big busybody. Whenever his name comes up in other people's conversations—and it often does—it's usually with all three names, slurred together, Mister Wendell Hardwick.

He owns umpteen miles of two-acre strips along the highways between Spokane and Boise. He owns all our brushes, the paint, a couple dozen scaffolds, a bazillion gallons of turpentine, and he owns us. Every first and third Saturday of every month. The pay is good, and our three fathers, all sons of Ralph Lundstrum, have agreed that *work* is good; work will bond us; work will keep us out of trouble; work will help us pay for college.

We hurry. The scaffold's getting slick, and the Chinook winds jostle it and the passing trains make it shimmy. The slickness only increases Jessie's goofiness. She dances past me, slipping and sliding, sticks her roller in the bucket, and dances back around me. When a wind comes up, Buster grabs hold of the ropes. "Wind, watch it," he says.

We all pause when the 3:08 to Whitefish goes by. Jessie smokes half a cigarette by the last of the billboard lady, a dark blue hip. She's gone white the rest of the way up. The train ascends, then disappears into the darkening east. It follows, in reverse, the course of glaciers. The little white rocks we'll flick out of our boot soles later tonight break open, and chips of ancient seashells fall out. From the old beach. A swath of the Mid-Cretaceous sea, I tell the others. It wasn't too far from here. Then, as often happens, the two girls say at the same moment and in a strangely perfect two-part harmony, "Shut-Up-Rob-Ert."

To Buster they offer sticks of Dentyne or an orange SweeTart. But only the orange ones. Both girls squinch their noses when they see that the next one in the roll is orange, and they pass the pack to Buster, who knows to take the top one.

Finished at last with the billboard, I drive us to the next place, and we set our white pails beneath the water tower. We crank up the radio loud. *Ziggy loves Teensy*: white. *Make war into love:*

whiter yet. Existential declarations. The statements retract as the night stars nose out into still one more sky of snow.

Done for the day, we load up and drive toward Von's, passing the park's pond, and Lynette says, "Oh, don't those ducks look like they've frozen right there?" Jessie curses the cheap paint and says she's sure it's toxic. Buster says, "Four white birds on the branch," and at first I think it's a joke about us, about our day in the wind, and then I see he's pointing out my window to actual birds.

Our fingers smell like turpentine. It's a smell that lives in us and will, I suspect, do so forevermore. Whatever, I think, one more year and I'll be graduated and out of this town. I'll climb up to this same water tower we just cleared of graffiti and with a few other guys paint some *fuck-you*'s and *Class of '74* in purple.

We pull up at Von's. Mr. Wendell Hardwick meets us at the step. He holds open the door for us. He smiles and waits. We don't hurry. We pile out and move toward him. He has no eyes. We see ourselves where the eyes should be: four white dots in his dark glasses.

⟲

The One-Eyed May Not Speak to the Captain

Lynette, age 40, 1997

What issues forth from the great ripped-open torso of the ferry: moths and butterflies. They make clots of color as they flutter ashore.

They who've disembarked are hell-bent on photographing anything picturesque. "O Canada" is more a sigh than a song. They've strapped on shiny black camera gear. They consult maps and devices that measure sunlight, water light, mountain light. Later, heading up the switchbacks, they resemble a colorful scaffolding, newly installed, to hold up the mountain.

Earlier the morning air had a sweetness of hedge roses and a damp, pent-up stillness that suggested at any coming moment a storm. But the morning passed, and no storm. Aunt Dot and Uncle Mel are to meet me, but they weren't sure which ferry they'd be able to catch. The first ferry comes and goes.

As soon as the ferrymen arrive, they plan for departure. Departing, they plan for arrival. They wear yellow rain slickers, even in perfectly good sunshine. Around the iron moorings, they coil ropes in figure eights—signs of infinity—then uncoil them.

Over the great wheel that turns the ferry is a sign of Don't Do's. Topping the list is Don't Speak to the Captain. But many people do. They ask to take his picture. They thank him for the lovely voyage. They offer him gum or chocolate. But he won't be gifted or thanked. He won't smile or speak or look a person in the eye. He stares toward arrival. He pulls up to the dock like Columbus confronting a new continent.

From the next ferry, Uncle Mel steps onto the dock, smiling. Aunt Dot follows behind, frowning. Her enormous black purse seems to weigh her down. They're going to decide what to do with me. Perhaps take me back across the border and deliver me to my own place in Spokane, or maybe take me way east to Montana, to the old Lundstrum family ranch, where Uncle Mel still goes twice a year to plant and later harvest hay. Or perhaps they'll take me to their other home, Grandpa Ralph's old cabin on Davis Lake, where Dot and Mel have been "camped" (their word) for thirteen years.

I've walked to the dock from the Willow Motel. Three and a half miles. My one eye sees double, and the other recognizes shapes . . . more or less. It's been a challenge to keep myself to the road's gravel edge and not step left into stumps or right, up onto the road itself, along which logging trucks loudly hurl themselves.

Recrossing Kootenay Lake, the ferrymen are already shrinking. By the time the boat veers around the jut of the northern shore, the crewmen appear to be swarming like yellow bees on a tiny hive.

Mel and Dot and I agree we won't decide anything too soon. The daylight is so bright. We soak in a hot spring in a cave, and when we come out, it is night. I'm newly in love with the night sky. Unbutton the mother-of-pearl buttons on her billowing black dress, and the widow is secretly happy. Luminous and alone. She only pretends to be mourning.

Aunt Dot hums as Uncle Mel drives us back to town. Spanning the river that endlessly feeds the lake, the bridge is lined with statues. Two centuries ago, a man used to come by and light acetylene in the stone wreaths that crown the statues' heads. This did nothing to calm the river below. Nothing's ever calmed it. For it, everything is transit, the water contorting itself—deeper, farther, harder—into more of itself.

A Kingdom Comes

Buster, age 3, 1960

Buster turned three in April. April 15. As his mother made a cake for him, his father sat at the kitchen table, bent over the tax form, erasing numbers and putting in new ones. "What the hell," he said finally, "I guess it's just one more check we can't cover."

"C'est la vie," his mother called, her head inside the fridge.

"Yeah, but this one's big," his father said, writing. "Big." Then he stopped. "Shit," he said and shook the pen.

"Watch it," his mother called. "Buster can hear, you know."

His father winked at him and smiled.

"He can add too, by the way," his mother said.

"You mean he can *count?*" His father looked over Buster's head. A wind was whipping loudly outside the patio doors.

Buster sat on the floor jamming together plastic spheres and cubes.

"No, he added something yesterday," his mother said. "Ask him three and three." She came and stood near the table.

"Hey, Buster, what's three and three?"

"Six," he said and pulled a black cone loose from a red cylinder.

"Excellent." His father glanced at his mother. "Boo-Boo's been teaching Yogi Bear how to add. That's my guess."

"He hasn't watched that for months," she said. "Buster, tell Dad what you think of Yogi."

"Lard butt! Lard butt!" Buster said and added a little clap of his hands.

"He doesn't get that talk from me!" His father frowned. Then he held up the checkbook ledger. "That sewing machine cost three hundred dollars?" he asked Buster's mother.

"I'm going to make curtains," she said.

"Three-*hundred*-dollar curtains?"

"We don't have time for this now, Carl." His mother opened a cabinet. "Your cake's almost done, kiddo," she called. "How many candles should I put on it?"

"Ten," Buster shouted.

"Hey, you're getting ahead of yourself," his father said. He tore a check out of the book. "There're some ugly numbers on this sucker," he told Buster. "You're so good at adding, what's eight plus nine plus seven?"

"Twenty-four," Buster said.

His father sat back in his chair. The wind outside rattled a garbage can. Buster worried that it would blow into the street and a big truck would come by and crush it. He'd seen a crushed garbage can in the street before.

"He got another one right," his father called.

"I told you," his mother said. She stood at the counter, licking white frosting off a spoon.

Buster got up and went to the sliding glass door. He put his hands exactly in the place of the handprints he'd made there yesterday. He hated it when his mother wiped them away. The pine trees blew wildly as if trying to rip themselves loose from the ground.

"What's forty-four plus sixty-seven?" his father asked.

"One one one," Buster told him. The wind seemed to be coming from beyond the Hallsteads' house, and Buster couldn't think what was over there to cause it.

"What?" his mother said and Buster turned. The spoon dangled from her hand, and when Buster reached for it, she let it slide from her fingers. She looked at his father. "That was right. Wasn't it?"

"He must be guessing," his father said.

"Wind," Buster told them. "*Szzz*," he said, trying to imitate the sound. He licked the spoon, but there was nothing on it.

"Okay, Buster," his mother asked, "what's eighty-four plus ninety-one?" She and his father were watching him as if he'd tried to hide his broccoli under his bread.

"One seven five," he told them. "How much is that?"

Now their faces seemed stretched out: the top halves happy and the bottom halves afraid.

"Where'd you learn those numbers, Sweetie?" his mother asked, and Buster thought her voice had a little not-nice edge to it.

Buster shrugged. "A thousand comes after the three nines," he said. He had trouble with the sound that started the word thousand. It was a sound they kept making him practice.

"Yes," his father said. "Right."

"Cake?" Buster asked him.

His mother stooped down and touched Buster's arm. "Tell Mommy, what is eight five zero nine plus seven seven six three?" She said each number slowly. "Write this down, Carl," she said to Buster's dad.

"We're going to have cake in one minute," his father said. "Can you say the number?" He looked up from the piece of paper he'd written on.

"One six two seven two." Buster pressed his palms together. "How big is that?" He turned toward his father. He felt he'd swung too high into the dense air of numbers.

"Very big," his mother said. She tied one of Buster's shoelaces. "I'm guessing that's right."

His father nodded. "It's over sixteen thousand."

The wind made another sound just then, like a high wail, and an aluminum garbage can lid banged against the mailbox outside. They all jumped.

"Come here, son," his father said and took Buster up into his lap.

Buster liked the lap, but now it seemed the cake might be postponed.

His mother went back to the cake. "The post office closes in a half-hour," she said. "I'm going to light these candles so Buster can blow them out, and then you can swing by the post office, and we'll have cake when you get back. How's that?"

His father's hand brushed the top of Buster's head. "How's that?" his father said into his ear.

"Good," Buster said.

When the cake came to the table, the candles made a soft hissing noise. Buster wasn't sure—he couldn't remember—did he have to eat them? He turned and looked at his father. "That's too much," he said.

"What?" his mother said. "Too much frosting?"

"Too much candles," Buster said and felt his eyes well up. He wanted to eat the cake, but now there was this error, this mistake that should be corrected.

"Yeah," his father said, seeing at last what Buster meant. "Mary—*what*?"

"No, no, the fourth candle is one to grow on," his mother said. "That's what we always did in my family."

"I'm *four*?" Buster said. He had grown *on*? The farther, longer numbers he didn't know the names of suddenly seemed somehow easier than these deadweight small ones. The four of them were burning up on the cake.

"No," his father said. "Mary, don't screw with the kid." His father picked a candle off the cake and aimed it at the sink.

Buster watched it sail across the room. Its little flame left a thin smoky trail.

"Okay, blow these out," his father said. "Dad has to run an errand. Take a big breath."

Where the fourth candle had been was a hole that made the cake look hurt. Buster stuck his pinky there.

"Hey," his mother said.

His father pulled Buster's hand away.

Just then: *Thwack!* The sliding glass door beside them was hit.

His father jumped, and Buster slid to the floor.

The garbage can lid, like a huge silver bug, was smashed against the glass. Then it rattled to the ground. And next—next came the great amazing moment of Buster's life. A spider-web pattern of cracks shot out in all directions from the gash at the center of the glass door.

"Don't get near that!" his mother shouted, and his father put a hand on Buster's head again, this time pressing down, holding Buster still.

He felt a happiness he hadn't known before. *Three, three, three* flashed in his mind—the number of intersections the cracks had made. The threes beat through him as a kind of pulse: pure and raw and powerful. A blast and a reckoning . . . as if the wind had spoken. Then he heard his name. But he closed his eyes against it. The threes flashed: magenta and gold and magenta. "Buster?" the life in the room called. "Buster," it said. "Come on, now. Time to blow out your candles."

He turned to it. There might have to be a birthday song before he could eat the snowy frosting.

Exactly thirty years later, Buster was the only one warm on the ice. An hour ago, when the electrician's toolbox had fallen sixty feet from a scaffold and hit the rink, Buster had hurriedly skated out there, exhilarated, hopeful. The show's manager, Mr. Merriman, in loafers, came and stood next to him. They both stared down at the deep gouge. Buster sighed, his joyous expectancy dissipating. No miraculous web pattern had radiated out yet—and now it seemingly never would. He knelt and ran his hands over the jagged crack. *Tedious* was the word he was thinking but knew better than to say.

"That divot's gotta be plugged," Merriman said. "There's always something, eh, Buster?"

Buster nodded. He knew the rink's Zamboni would have to come back and make a few more passes to resurface the bad place. He picked up the toolbox and handed it to Merriman. "Always something," he said.

Buster skated the rink's circumference, watching Beauty out of the Beast's eyeholes. Beauty barely spoke to him, and when she did, it wasn't English. Not quite. Her skates she called *scats.* At that moment she was going through her elaborate ritual of lacing the *scats.* She'd made a mistake and had to start all over with the loop and cross and tug. During performances, with the house lights off and Beauty in his raised paws in the air, she'd turn her head and look at him—and *terror!* But it was terror, Buster knew, helped along by black eyeliner and the flushed cheeks that came in a plastic tube. Over his head and on her back, Beauty's skates pointed straight up, and her gown fell across his hideous snout. Oh bad Beast, put her down, the children moaned in the stands. Bad, bad Beast, don't drop her.

He'd never dropped her. He doubted he even *could* drop her. Like a cat, she always landed on her feet, although sometimes not precisely as she liked, and then there'd be hissed Ukrainian profanities. Ten years ago she'd skated in the Olympics, and she still held herself to her former competence.

The marred ice had delayed their practice. But it hardly mattered. The practice was primarily to get a feel for the rink of a new town. But this town, Spokane, for Buster, wasn't new. It was *his* town. And like every year, his father would be in the audience. He'd see his mother when the show went to Tacoma, where she lived now with her boyfriend Stan.

Picking up speed, Buster skated backward: crossover, leap, half-camel. The rink, in his mind's eye, was a silver zero he dissected at erratic angles. The Beast-body required surrender. The great jaws opened, and the fangs flashed. The Beast was mostly muscle. Thoughts and half-thoughts flitted by. He flipped over himself. He spun. For a few seconds the world rushed by. It had a swelling music piped in to accompany it.

During performances, there was a moment each night when he stood motionless at the edge of the rink, pretending to watch Beauty sail around the ice, but really glancing into the grandstands and tallying the audience. He and Merriman had a standing bet on how close he could get: ten bucks if he was within ten. He didn't exactly "count." He looked and took in the heads—rows of pale dots crossing a dark screen. Last night it was 709. He'd hit it on the nose, which made Merriman laugh when he laid the ten-spot across the tattered paw.

"He's still the best spinner in the biz," Merriman had told Buster's father last year after the show. Buster had seen videotapes of himself. In his spin, he was a blur of brown fur.

"How many times did you spin?" his father had asked him once when he was twelve. His skates had been too tight that year, but he'd have to wait another year for new ones.

"I lost count," Buster told him.

"You? You never lose count," his father said.

When he and his father skated on Davis Lake, their silver blades made the sound of doors opening on squeaky hinges.

"I'll try again," Buster had said. But inside his spin, Buster lost his focus. The tall pine with the dead black branch on top swirled into the greens and blues around the frozen lake. He'd laugh when he stepped out of the spin. There were no numbers in there—only the prismatic afterimages of colors. "Sorry," he told his dad, breathing in the cold air. He had the sense even then that the spin was somehow connected to who he was, or to who he would become.

"I think it must have been over thirty," his father said.

"Your guess is as good as mine," Buster told him.

When Beauty skated out to the cracked place, she frowned at it and shook her head. "*Derka*," she called it. "No good."

"Always something," he told her.

Beauty has told her sister, Mitka, their makeup person, to tell Buster he needs to develop his people skills. Mitka just laughs when she translates this for Buster.

In the story he and Beauty are supposed to be from, he was born a prince of Persia, but fled to France as a young man and got involved with Beauty and a rose garden and a mischievous pet fox. There was little sense to the plot. A prince turns into a monster and then back into a man. Only the children seemed to get it. To all the world, the Beast's roar sounds as if it comes from the gaping mouth. But no. It's prerecorded. It comes from a sound booth. Buster holds open the spring of the jaws with his own mouth. Someone presses a button: the roar sounds. The Beast skates toward origin: less fur around a princely heart. The Beast has to believe there will come a time; there will come a kingdom.

There was a boy too, a real boy, Kenny, who was five. Kenny could start a sentence in Ukrainian and finish it in English. Sometimes he ran out onto the ice, and Buster chased him, lifted him, and pulled him close into a spin, making the boy shriek with delight. Kenny's mother was Beauty's sister, Mitka, who was the true beauty. She had even gone to beauty school. In Miami. And her English was good. Once, when Buster had been lost in numbers flipping by on a gas pump, she'd stepped out of the van and spoken to him. He'd felt trapped by a broken five that went round and round. He jumped when she spoke. "And we need diapers too," she said and touched his arm. It pleased him the way she did this—forcing him out of and past a bad moment. Mitka helped him pass as an ordinary man. He liked to kiss her five times when they woke in the morning. Four or six was incorrect. This she never questioned.

Beauty, whose real name is Sophie, likes the numbers that make ratios. She reads them from magazines to Buster: *ten chickens every one second lose a head; three of five children living now in America is hungry.* She knows where the battles are in the world and tells Buster the numbers of the missing, dead, and wounded. Deep in a particular corner of his mind, he's kept a running total, although he doubts it's even close. Sophie's eyes scan here and there, but just in the Ukrainian and Russian papers, the only ones she can read.

Buster's father watched from row two, the center aisle, but Buster, skating by, couldn't make out the words in black ink on his father's T-shirt. Later, backstage, after the show, he does: *Grandpa's my name, spoiling's my game.* Buster has to explain it to Mitka, who translates it once for Sophie, checks again with Buster on the meaning of *spoiling,* finds another word, and re-explains it.

Through all of this, Buster, his father, and Kenny stand calmly watching the two lovely women, waiting for the moment they'll get the joke and their chins will tilt back in laughter. But that doesn't happen. Sophie, still in her Princess of Persia tiara, finally nods at the T-shirt and kisses Buster's father on both cheeks, which makes him grin.

His father says he has a little boat now, and tomorrow, since it's a non-show day, he'll take them out on a big lake. When he says the name of the lake, Coeur d'Alene, Beauty frowns.

"*Coeur* d'Alene," she repeats, pronouncing it in what Buster assumes is better French.

His father tries it her way, although it's not the way the locals say it.

But the next day starts out with a cold rain, and Buster suggests that they drive up to the small lake, Davis Lake, where his father still lives. Sophie stays behind to get a facial, and the others pile into his father's pickup—Mitka in the middle and Kenny on Buster's lap—and head straight north. They pass the waterfall over the Spokane River, which he has always remembered as the number seven. Elevens are grass widows. The number one is a white birch tree near the lake bank. A boy walking backward in a meadow is nine. The landscape never completes its arithmetic. A leaf falls, a cricket leaps, and all must be retabulated. Years ago, this too-muchness could make him bury his face in his hands.

Years ago he had crept about the earth, trembling. Once there had been a pain deep in his belly, and although he had moaned and called out *Help me, help me,* he hadn't known what was inside him, or how to speak of it. He'd gone into a dark sleep in which he felt himself being smothered. He woke surrounded by white ghosts. He'd been afraid of them—until he realized they weren't lifting his life away from the earth, they were keeping him on it. They were saving him. It took him a long time to realize this, although he'd heard it five times coming through his father's voice. Buster wasn't sure, though. He couldn't at first quite trust the face or the words; his father spoke from behind a green cloth mask, which Buster later understood was to ensure that he didn't breathe out any germs that Buster shouldn't breathe in.

Buster's appendix had burst. He was nine years old. It was the year his teachers had told his parents he didn't have much chance of being mainstreamed anymore beyond that year, fourth grade. He'd need to go into special ed. They'd said he was reading all right, and of course his math was, well, frighteningly good, but he showed little acknowledgment of other people. He turned away if spoken to. He liked to mimic the tick-tock of a clock or the weather's sounds, the patter of rain, for instance. The teachers told his parents they didn't think they could help prepare him for the real business of ordinary life. All of this news had made his mother cry, late at night, when she thought Buster was asleep. His father had tried to hush her, as if she were the child. *It'll be okay,* his father said. *We'll find a way.*

But the nurses—that spring when the appendix burst and sent a shock of poison through him—did not know any of this about Buster. Bending over him, laying the pale specters of their palms on his head, they thought he was a regular kid. *We almost lost you, little guy,* the dark-eyed one had whispered. *But look, you're still here. You're still with us.*

The wind, Buster heard it outside the hospital room. And then he knew: the wind was *outside.* And he was right there, *inside.* He was with the people in the white clothes. The wind was the breath of space. Empty space. He was here, in a room of bodies bent to the ministrations of bodies. He was a body too. He was alive among the living.

He raised himself to his elbows. "Thank you," he said to the nurses.

"Well, aren't you dear?" said the one with the gold glasses. "Hey, Georgine, he's finally talking," she spoke out the door into the echoing hallway.

"I'm here," he said, as if his teacher had called his name on the roll and he had, at last, raised his hand.

By the time they reach Davis Lake, the weather is clear and sunny. The cabin and its contents are completely unchanged. Buster is sure even the yellow-flowered dishtowel is the same. There is still the table that was once a door and a lamp made out of what were once elk antlers. Buster's dad opens two cans of tomato soup and puts a pot on the woodstove.

When Mitka asks about Buster's mother's photo, still in a frame by the bathroom door, his father calls from the kitchen, "That's all water under the bridge, honey."

"What bridge?" Kenny asks him.

"The *old* bridge," Buster's father says.

Kenny nods as if the unexpected answer is surprising only because of its obviousness.

"You can stir the soup, Ken, but be careful not to touch the stove."

Buster recognizes in his father's voice the old steady tenderness. He takes Middy's hand. His heart feels like the heart of a prince.

After lunch, the four of them walk around the lake. Mitka is fascinated with the wildflowers—so brightly blooming—among the field grasses. *Coneflowers, larkspur:* Buster tells her their names, and she tells Kenny what they're called in Ukrainian. For Kenny, everything is twice named. Buster can't fathom how the boy keeps it all straight. He guesses that Middy is just making up these words for the flowers anyway. She hates for there not to be some equivalent from her homeland.

Grandfather is *Dida*. He, Buster, is *Dad* and also *Tato*.

Last night he told Kenny about the eagles on Davis Lake he'd watched as a boy. Sometimes if there was an early spring freeze, a few napping ducklings might find themselves frozen into the ice. That was when an eagle swooped down and flew off with a duckling dangling from its talons. Buster remembered skating by a cluster of what looked like popsicle sticks poking up through the ice. Those, he told Kenny, were the ducks' legs. Just the legs. Kenny laughed. He'd heard that story a dozen times, and each time he laughed.

Buster had made up his mind that on this trip home he would finally tell his father the secret of his only grandson: that Kenny is *not* from him and Mitka, that Kenny is from Detroit. Kenny is from the Joe Louis Arena in Detroit, Michigan. The story they'd told his father five years ago—of Mitka and Buster creating Kenny out of their young love—that was a lie. They'd made it up in a girls' bathroom on a snowy Michigan night. But now, as if by a surprise unfolding of some god's formerly closed fist, now he and Mitka were married, and now there was to be a baby from them after all. The new child was just beginning to live inside Mitka. The truth of this news somehow made the old lie impossible. Maybe they wouldn't tell Merriman the truth. Maybe they'd not bother Buster's mother with it. But he, Buster, would at last say what was true to his father.

"I've been meaning to tell you about this bad night in Detroit five years ago," he started. He and his father were sitting at the top of a small hill. At the bottom Mitka and Kenny were gathering a bouquet. Kenny pulled up grasses and pine needles and handed them to Mitka. Buster explained first about how the Detroit ice show had been over for hours and the audience was long gone, and that Mitka and Sophie—passing a girls' lavatory and hearing a loud moaning in there—had gone inside. They saw a girl's legs—splayed open on the floor—under one of the stalls. *Oh god oh god oh god,* the girl was saying. There'd been a lot of blood. As Buster was telling this part of the story, he saw a flock of red-winged blackbirds alight—thirty-seven of them—in two half-dead cottonwoods, but he didn't pause from the narration. He was, he told his father, the one Mitka and Sophie had found first when they'd run for help. And as he said that, he realized it could just as easily have been Merriman; it could have been a security guard. Anyone.

When Buster had entered the bathroom, everything was loud and fast and the Ukrainian blurred into the American *oh gods,* and there, suddenly, was a baby, and Mitka had her hands around the tiny bloody head and was tugging. *Is it dead?* Sophie had asked in perfect English so that Buster would have to answer, so that Buster would lean down and open the baby's lips, Kenny's lips, and wipe away the bloody sac and watch the boy open his eyes—eyes shocked and horrified by the faces leaning over him, staring as he took in his first breath so as to be able to let go his first scream.

Sophie left and came back with a box knife and handed it to Middy, who cut the cord. Sophie would help them make up the entire story later, when the girl was gone, and they were huddled there holding a baby that Buster said could not, absolutely *not*, as Sophie suggested, be called Detroit.

All this Buster told his father. He said the girl had been angry about the blood on her clothes. *How am I supposed to go home like this* were the first words she'd said when she sat up and looked down at her skirt. He told his father that the girl had washed herself as Middy wrapped the baby in paper towels. The baby was red-faced, crying high-pitched wails. Middy pushed the child toward the girl. Then she and Sophie washed their hands. Buster too. They stood at the bank of sinks washing, watching in the mirror as the girl stared down at the baby. The girl had long black hair with green streaks. There was blood on her tall black boots. She frowned at the wriggling baby. Then she picked it up, stood slowly, and walked to the doorway. There she stopped and set the baby—now howling—in the trash container, which was already overflowing with paper towels. She turned, stared at the three of them at the sinks, and shook her head. Then she was gone. The baby, bundled in paper towels, sank, second by second, more deeply into the huge mess of them.

Mitka went over and picked him up. Tears were flowing down Sophie's cheeks.

"I bet that girl had no idea who you three were," his father said. "You weren't in costume, were you?"

"No, no costumes."

"So she couldn't even come looking for you later if she changed her mind."

"I doubt she'd change it," Buster said. "I doubt it was a changeable mind."

His father drew a long breath as if he'd been the one speaking. Then he slowly shook and shook his head.

He and Buster stared down the hill at Middy and Kenny. Once, out here on this very hill, his father had said, "Listen, Buster, we just need to get back on our feet." It was a phrase his father had said many times that first winter in Grandpa Ralph's cabin. Grandpa stayed in town, as usual, in a brick house. Buster's mother said no one who wasn't crazy would live out here past October. If the woodstove in the kitchen weren't stoked all night, the pipes would freeze. His mother swore at those pipes, swore at the cold toilet and at the crèche on the mantle with its sleeping lambs bigger than the wise men. "Don't let a meter maid put a ticket on the car," his father had told him on a trip to town that winter. "Just say your dad'll be back in a sec." Buster sat in the car staring at the roof of the bank building into which his father had gone. A line of wooden soldiers marched, all lit up. The lights made their legs go up and down in a logarithmic pattern of shifting twelves. The soldiers had drums and flutes but made no sound. They seemed to march toward a throbbing Christmas tree but never quite arrived.

After a long time, Buster's father came out of the bank and stood on the sidewalk. He opened a white handkerchief and passed it over his eyes and forehead. A light snow was falling, and the flakes melted when they landed on his brown wool coat. Buster wasn't sure then, or now, but when his father glanced down the street, blinking, he no longer seemed to know where the car was, where Buster was, how to get from point A of Old National Bank to point B, Buster and the car. Buster put his hand on the car's windshield. His father looked up, nodded, and crossed the street.

Buster tells his father he said no that night in Detroit—many no's—to the sisters. Middy had gone out and come back with diapers and cans of formula, and soon it was dawn and Sophie had kissed the baby and Buster had held him, and Middy had said *Tato* so sweetly, and Buster was out of breath and had no more no in him. They'd be all the way to Chicago, or farther, Middy said, before Merriman had to find out about the baby, and they'd just say it was strange he hadn't realized how fat Mitka had gotten. They'd ask how he'd failed to notice all the big sweaters she'd been wearing. They'd explain x, y, and z—Sophie adding a few phrases in Ukrainian, Middy subtracting, and Buster retotaling. The lie had been a group effort, but it felt good to be done with it now. And there, Buster thought, endeth the story of how a boy had come to live in the Beast's world.

They flew into dawn, through a compressed day, then a rushed twilight, and finally the former Soviet Union lay below them: darkly verdant. The sisters were happy. They were to be welcomed back. Only a few years ago, they would not have been. For so long, Sophie told Kenny, they had been *persona non grata*. Kenny took the third language in stride and went on eating Cheerios out of a plastic bag. The show was on a two-month hiatus. He of the fang and claw—the one so lovingly hated, so joyfully booed—was on a break. No more of that sliding-on-his-knees maneuver when he released his Beauty from her bondage, received her kiss, and let the audience linger in the dreamy lie that the barbarism of the twenty-first century had slipped away at the moment he unzipped, stepped out of a

One-Eyed but Seeing What the Pines Are Now

Lynette, age 40, 1997

From the pasture, the five brown horses came to stand with me at the fence. We watched the new black horse jump hurdles, carrying a rider—a girl in a white helmet and tall tan boots. When she and the horse sailed over the rails and dropped down, the five brown horses stomped and whinnied and threw their heads.

The stable boys, my brother Robert's old high school friends, kept shoveling. They used to be paperboys. They used to walk poodles. Now they work extra hours to support cars that sit on concrete blocks and drip and rust and stink.

Mid-morning, and the moon's punched-in face was ghostly and low when the new black horse slid up under it.

Dust in our eyes. Me and the old horses. Twelve wide brown eyes staring. The girl, the rider, had that white helmet—like a cartoon bubble waiting for words above the horse's head.

Hey now, Lynnie, the boys called to me. *Look at them lilies you threw out.* They pointed. *I tried,* I called back. And I had. I'd tried getting rid of those lilies. But now they'd sprouted—chartreuse shoots—in all directions from the mound of last year's manure and weeds and old tomato vines.

The new horse circled and came around, heading fast toward another jump. At the fence we heard him snorting as he passed. His rider urging *Good boy, Good boy* into his ear.

If the horse made this jump, a black arc—appearing like some suddenly simplified abstract Truth—would widen and hang in the air. The horse's four white feet would fling it off the ground. Something the brown horses and I couldn't believe we'd believe, but we would. We did.

One day last year, the boys drank themselves silly and drove into trees, though they rarely speak of it. Shrugging if they're asked. *What-ever.* The next week they brought saws and turned those trees into these hurdles.

A great black girth soon to be poised in the air over them. There. Like God's eyebrow raised.

The rich girl with her head low, saying she knows he can do it, *Good boy,* and the other horses all look up and me too, and we expect him to do it, and the boys pause a minute and smoke and nod once at Good Boy . . . as he does it.

We let out our held breaths. Then I pound a sagging fence rail back into its nail. Even after all these years, I still carry a hammer in my handbag. This is a thing the boys tell their girl-friends in the dark.

The Wild Boys

Jessie, age 12, 1971

It wouldn't be the first time. That's what Jessie kept thinking. She was sure her heart would break, but *it wouldn't be the first time*. Where was that cousin Deedee? Where was she now?

When Jessie was twelve and Lynette thirteen, they'd been flown to Florida to visit their Aunt Mary. Divorced by then from Uncle Carl for six years, she had a new family in Florida: a foster daughter named Deedee who was fourteen and a new little girl, Kiki.

"Are they our cousins too?" Jessie had asked her Aunt Dot, who was now her mother.

Dot had to think for a minute. "Semi-cousins, let's say. Mel and I—and Aunt Cheryl and Uncle Hank too—we want our families to stay connected with Mary."

"Right," her father had added. "After all, Aunt Mary's still Buster's mother. She'll always be his mother."

Down there in Florida, Jessie and Lynette, along with the semi-cousins Deedee and Kiki, spent balmy days on the white sands of Pine Island Key. Each night Jessie held her arm up close to Lynette's arm, comparing the new shades of pink, next a sweet peachy tan, then the deepening brown. Deedee knew just how much and then how little suntan lotion she and Lynette and even tiny Kiki needed.

Dropped off at the beach for the day, the four girls hurried past all the beachgoers, gawking at the semi-nude German couples kissing deeply, their mouths making sucking sounds, the women's huge sagging breasts heaving under bikini tops. The girls barely glanced at the ridiculous old couples eating bologna on white bread. And they rushed past the boys their own age, ordinary boys snorkeling and laughing too loud. Such boys warranted but the briefest glance.

Though their feet carried them only to the far end of Settlers' Beach, in their minds they went farther: across the black jagged rocks where the anole lizards sunned, whipping their tails around themselves, puffing out the red sacs in their necks, and then farther still: over the rocks honeycombed with sinkholes, rocks on which gators slept with one eye open, the rocks where they knew the wild, completely off-limits boys were hiding.

One day Deedee sat up, staring toward the black rocks, and let down the straps of her bikini top. Then Lynette did the same. And then Jessie did. There were bruises on Deedee's arms, which Jessie and Lynette would glance at and then quickly look away. They watched the waves. The white froth was high. Little Kiki kept busy burying the older girls' feet in the sand, which was warm and as fine as salt.

Jessie would later wonder if she and Lynette had only dreamed that place, those girls, their purple flip-flops. Jessie and Lynette had been briefly dropped down into that world and then just as briefly snatched away. As Jessie grew older, she'd felt it her duty to remind Lynette—and each year with increasing solemnity—of Deedee, poor Deedee. She'd been a runaway before she came to live with Aunt Mary. And for all they knew, she was again. She was still. Poor Deedee. Even into their late twenties, Jessie and Lynette each kept a small gold-framed photo of Deedee in a bedside drawer, near the locked diaries and confirmation crucifixes that were made of petrified wood from a great lost redwood forest.

Deedee and Kiki, who was five, lived in a house up on stilts with Aunt Mary and a black-haired father who always wore a crisp white uniform. In back of their house, a canal of warm saltwater ran like an alley. Kiki could at any moment suddenly run down the dock and jump into it. *It* was the ocean.

The sand was hot hot hot on their feet. Jessie said this each time during the phone conversations home to Mel and Dot, her still relatively new parents, who'd taken her in after the first heartbreak, the obliteration of her own family.

"Holy cow, we were born for the beach," she'd tell them. Mel would be laughing on one line, and Lynette's parents on the other line, and all of them reminding Jessie and Lynette to "pick up after yourselves, girls; don't cause Mary any grief."

But they hardly saw Aunt Mary. She waited tables at night, slept late, and of course all day the girls were gone. Deedee's foster father, Chief Petty Officer Kincaid, worked for the Coast Guard, and on his way to work, in his big white convertible, he'd deliver the four girls to the beach. He'd pick them up at five. Exactly. He'd lay on the horn if they were one minute late. Jessie, Lynette, and the quasi-cousins would pile in with their beach towels, bottles of baby oil (with iodine in it to stain their skin darker), Kiki's bucket and shovels, and everyone's sunglasses, everyone's hairbrushes and flip-flops, and the now-empty plastic jug that had held their fruit punch.

The boys were why the girls went to the beach. The boys were wild. They had, Deedee said, turned savage. They were Deedee's age but living amid tangled mangrove roots, hiding from the authorities. They'd been on their own so long—untouched by the stink of curfews and Sunday dinners—they were completely alone unto themselves, answerable to no one, dependent on nothing.

Deedee pointed them out: just around the jut of rocks where the white sand ended and the rough black stones met the water. Jessie understood that the boys no longer carried within them whatever it was that kept her and the other girls swimming, as instructed, under the lifeguard's watch, within the rim of white buoys. Jessie looked toward the rocks, shielding her eyes from the afternoon sun. A dozen boys, Deedee said. Maybe more. Maybe twenty.

Agile on the rocks, the boys fished for yellowfin. Sometimes the girls thought they could smell it grilling on fires far off in the buttonwood sloughs. Chief Kincaid said he'd sent out five Coast Guard men in green canoes to find those fires and the boys who tended them. The canoes had gone in but never returned.

Chief Kincaid called the boys hooligans. He'd been working with his Coast Guard crew for years to catch them. Officer Kincaid, in his spotless white shoes and his dark hair cut straight across the back of his neck, towered over the girls, over everybody. One night while the four girls waded in the canal behind Deedee's house, he suddenly appeared and jerked Deedee out of the water. Jessie and Lynette stared as he gripped her arm. "Dishes," he shouted. "I told you hours ago. Inside. Now."

Jessie and Lynette climbed out and sat on the dock. They flicked canal water on their sunburned bellies. There was more shouting from inside. Aunt Mary was home, and her voice was shrill. Kiki braided Jessie's hair into a tangled hank. One of the girls—had it been Lynette? or Jessie herself?—mimicked what Mel always said about catching more flies with honey. A pasty moon had been rising. Why, Jessie wondered, would vinegar even be an option for flies? Then the three girls on the dock had gone silent, trying to catch what the screamed words were that came rushing toward them from inside the house. Jessie and Lynette had fought with their parents too, but never like that. The venom unnerved them.

After they'd seen the boys, it was as if the boys accompanied them everywhere—into endless conversations along the waterfront, or later, after sundown, as the girls paraded themselves up and down the streets, marveling at the houses on stilts, which, Deedee explained, helped them withstand the hurricane waters that rushed under and around, and allowed the people inside to be spared.

Wrapped in sun and buffed by sand, Jessie and Lynette ticked off their Florida days. They had that brief time of feeling sleek and knowing what lay on the other side of those white buoys. Kiki, standing up to her knees in the ocean, wearing a yellow sand bucket on her head, its wire handle under her chin, would scream if she saw a jellyfish—her *ooo, ooo, ooo* sailing toward them until Deedee would get up and go rap on her bucket helmet like a drum. *Shut-up, shut-up, shut-up.* Then Kiki would start to shake her hips to the tune, her mouth picking up the song's words. *Shut-up* meant Deedee was right there next to her. And sometimes Deedee would kick a chunk of seaweed into the foam. Something that only looked like a jellyfish. Something that only a child would fear.

Of course, all of this the wild boys would be watching. The girls wore their dark glasses so the boys wouldn't see them watching back. And as the days passed, the boys came closer. Each day a step or two nearer along the rocks. They threw shells into the water, and the brown pelicans, confused by the little splashes, swooped down. The boys had tied their long hair back with weeds—tangles of brown and gold and red, the colors mingling, swirling over their dark shoulders. The boys spoke a language they'd made up to suit their needs—whispered words the civilized world had no use for, words the girls tried to imagine and pronounce, syllables they couldn't get their tongues around. None of them could say how they'd speak to the boys if they ever got close enough.

And they did try to get closer. But if they walked a yard or two farther each day toward the rocks, Kiki was sure to follow, always staying just behind, shouting each girl's name in turn. Saying *Wait!* She was their shadow, a reminder of who they were, who they'd been, and where they'd come from.

Sometimes, lying in their separate dark silences as a muggy night quickly enveloped all of Big Pine Key, they saw the boys' faces—eyes as turquoise as the sea—and they felt the boys touch them, lightly, and open them . . . their most secret places exposed to the July moonlight pouring through the windows.

The girls were always preparing to go or preparing to return. *To* the beach. *From* the beach. The cool breezes were a balm on their raw sunburns. Riding home in the front seat next to the Chief, Deedee never forgot to read the road sign aloud, the one that greeted them after they'd crossed the channel bridge: Total Key Deer Killed This Year—37. On days the number increased, everyone would be silent the rest of the way home. Or sometimes Jessie would lift her hand and point out the window. *There,* she'd say, *is that one?* And everyone would turn and see one of the tiny deer that lived nowhere else in the world but this key. Deedee would rotate completely around from the station wagon's front seat to watch, as long as possible, a deer—smaller than a collie—nibbling grass near the highway. The Chief at the wheel never slowed down. Jessie would never forget: a fawn's hoofprints in the sand were the size of dimes.

On their last day there, little Kiki had buried Jessie's toes in the sand. Gray clouds filmed the sky. Big winds swirled. Off in the distance, the wild boys were rowing, their boats gliding between rock jetties, then disappearing under hanging boughs. Having buried Jessie's feet and then her legs, Kiki had moved on to Deedee, who just lay back on the sand and closed her eyes. Clearly she'd been buried a hundred times and knew how to settle in the sand. Jessie and Lynette looked at each other. Two wide lavender bruises, like careless paintbrush strokes, flared on the inside of Deedee's thighs. They'd seen the ones on her arms before: the petals of fingerprints.

Kiki smoothed the damp sand down over Deedee's feet, then up her legs. Kiki carried up buckets of water, buckets of sand. She was all business, and finally, finally those thighs were covered too. When Deedee asked for her sunglasses, Jessie had to put them on her; Deedee's arms were already buried.

"Let's go, Deedee," Jessie said.

"It's almost five," Lynette said. She had the waterproof watch.

"No. Y'all just go."

"But the tide," they said.

The pelicans screeched and swooped. The beach was emptying fast. The dyed black ends of Deedee's auburn hair stuck up from the sand like the spiky tendrils of an exotic vine.

"But the sand ants," Kiki pleaded.

Deedee was just a face in black sunglasses. The face told the girls again to go on and just leave her. The girls were to tell the Chief she was sick and had gotten a ride home already with a neighbor from down the street.

Kiki had begun putting a few rocks around Deedee—to show the wild boys, Kiki said, where Deedee's feet and hands were. Her limbs seemed barely discernible mounds that the water would soon flatten. The boys, Kiki told us, had food—shark steaks and coconut milk. Clearly Kiki was on board with the whole idea. But Jessie and Lynette weren't. They'd begged. One of them—hadn't it been Jessie?—cried. Suddenly

◎

The Twelfth District

Buster's mother, Mary, 1958

We were going to greet the man we wanted as our president. We had high hopes, although he wasn't even governor yet. To be honest, I had a little crush on him, and when I told my husband that, he said, "Good, Mary. Good for you."

He took my elbow and helped me walk across the slick frosted grass in my clunky winter boots. The crowd kept to the city park's sidewalks, but we didn't. We veered around anyone moving slowly. I was carrying the baby in a sling (a recent sewing project) against my chest, and the baby's head kept nodding between waking and sleeping.

"You're not serious about the crush, right?" Carl said.

"No, I don't think I'm serious."

"But are you willing to knock on doors for him? That's the real test of love."

"Depends on what neighborhood," I said.

Carl pointed. Ahead of us was our man, Wendell Hardwick, getting out of a black Chevy truck. Immediately people with cameras and microphones engulfed him. Carl and I queued up in the handshake line. Hardwick, who seemed taller in person, grasped people's hands and lifted them into the air. There was a feeling of a tidal wave of hands rising toward us.

The baby was suddenly quite awake. The cheering crowd had roused him, and his eyes darted about. He was seven months old. Awake, he wanted to take in everything. He was greedy for the world.

When Hardwick saw the baby, he nodded to him, brushed past a few well-wishers, and suddenly stood before me. I lifted Buster from his sling. Later Carl would say he was sure Buster had smiled at our man, the candidate for whom, through a month of phone calls, we'd raised nearly $20,000 from our financially strapped Twelfth District. Hardwick held out his hands to take my son, and I put him into those hands.

Buster, raised like the host over the pope's head, stared down at us, unflinching, as his cheeks—one, then the other—received their kiss. Flashbulbs popped. Then Buster blinked. The blinking eye was a blaze of green, the color of sea foam. It's the color of the sky I dive into in a dream. Hardwick's smile that cold November day was wider than Buster's whole face.

Beside me Carl cheered. I recall the elbow of Hardwick's navy jacket coming toward me, but someone had gotten in front of me, and I couldn't get my hands free to reach up and take the baby as Hardwick passed him down to me. And although Hardwick would later say he'd been sure my hands were right there—right there where they'd been only seconds before—they weren't. I accept that.

I recall the gasps. A woman's short, shrill scream. Then quiet, and a space opened like a shaft into a mine. There were several long moments as Hardwick and I knelt over Buster, who had fallen to the ground. I touched his throat to see if he had a pulse. Then I slipped my palm behind his head and picked him up as if lifting him from his crib. "Bus," I said. "Oh my god. Buster." I couldn't look at the tall figure in the navy coat. I couldn't look away from the closed eyes of my child.

Behind me Carl was shouting.

Then Hardwick stood and shouted the same thing. "Call an ambulance. Somebody call an ambulance. Please."

"Is he breathing?" Carl asked me, his voice both too loud and too whispery at the same time. I thought then that it would be Carl rather than me who would keel over right there in Lilac City Park if Buster died.

And then what would I do? What . . . then?

Hardwick's apology came at us in a tinny voice, not the deep voice we were used to, the one that had made bold promises about our rivers and schools. Carl and I had climbed into the back of the ambulance, and out of Hardwick's mouth and up to us came the word *sorry*, but not the true *sorry*, not *sorry* with the force of conviction, not the *sorry* we'd believe.

Hardwick called the hospital several times through our long night there. The nurses put Carl on the phone, and I heard him repeat what the doctors had said: babies are resilient. "We don't know yet," Carl told Hardwick. Carl's face was blank, his eyes on me, holding me in place like a moth stuck through with a pin. "They have to run tests," he told Hardwick. "Then we'll see."

I turned and stared out a window, watching the aluminum factory spewing silver smoke across the river. Buster had been whisked off to X-ray. The gray day became the black night with a dim sickle moon.

For two days "The Dropped Baby" might as well have been a TV show—picked up by the major networks, played on the morning and evening news. Aired, we'd heard, in Brazil. In the footage a stunned Wendell Hardwick waves the crowd back. "Watch out," he calls with great authority. "Don't step on the baby." There I am kneeling, the top of my head, my ponytail askew. Then Buster—Buster lying on the ground like a puddle of melting ice.

There are only so many times a person can watch her baby fall, slipping through a crack in the crowd. There are only so many times a mother can think that any poor grade on a spelling test, or a bedwetting at 3 A.M., must have resulted from this, this moment of the tiny body hitting the unforgiving ground. And everywhere there'd been plenty of hands, so many hands . . . reaching. And still this slippage. This fall.

Probably no one would say that Buster was fine. But he was okay. Carl taught him to ice-skate and row a boat on our small lake. There were geese down there, and sometimes Buster would bring me an egg and I'd make us an omelet. He was a sweet boy, average in school. Except for math. His facility for multiplying fractions was, his third grade teacher told us, quite beyond the national norm. *Any* national norm.

I wondered if in later life he'd come to know how I'd held him in my arms, and then hadn't. And knowing that, might he slip deeper into his solitude and I into mine?

Wendell Hardwick did not become our president. He never set foot in the governor's mansion. But he wrote us once, about a year after the accident. He asked after Buster's health and said again how sorry he was. He mentioned that he'd had a rough year himself; he'd gone back to ranching, and his cattle had recently been "blighted by a virus."

I read those words and folded the letter away beneath some socks. I was glad he'd never be our president. The air that morning at Lilac City Park had been bitter cold, and I'd hoped the handsome Mr. Hardwick might drape an arm around my shoulders, and Carl's too, that he'd thank us for believing in him. I'd called hundreds of people. I'd told them they'd be helping to usher in a bright future for our state, or some such baloney. Our district was full of lumbermen with no more trees to cut, silver miners with no more ore to mine.

A few weeks after the accident, I caught a look at Hardwick's plummeting poll numbers on TV and felt nothing. Now when I think of him, I see him following emaciated, weepy-eyed cattle. Down in the scablands of our state's southernmost valley, they shuffle toward a darkening sky. Hooves kick up a cloud of gritty dust, and Wendell Hardwick walks into it.

One-Eyed in Ab-So-Lutely, a Time of Too Much Money

Lynette, age 40, 1997

I loved seeing the Russian girl in my red and navy plaid suit. Years ago those crosshatched stripes had made me dizzy when I stared down at my knees. The skirt was too short. I didn't like seeing my own knees, though this girl's were nice—not knobby. She and her friend walked past me. This was near the end of the era of my old glasses, and I could see quite well the place where the skirt's hem had come loose, making one side sag so the girl seemed to walk at a tilt.

American adjectives—*stellar, hilarious, kid-you-not*—punctuated the girls' hurried Russian. They'd come out of the crumbling old church where the day before I'd dropped off three boxes of clothes—boxes I could barely see over and had to carry, slowly, one by one, down the broken stairs into a cellar rank with mildew. Setting the first box down, I saw why: damp hymnals in teetering towers against one wall.

The last time I'd been in that church was to bid farewell to my former boss from the Chef's Pal, Mr. Kinney. I'd heard the mortician ask the florist's girl to move a spray of yellow roses up over Mr. Kinney's hands. *The* hands was what the mortician had said.

The backs of Mr. Kinney's hands—bruised blue and purple-black from the IV needles—were not the sort of thing mourners wanted to see.

None of us could manage to sing over the loud organ music. Or perhaps the sight of the kind-hearted Mr. Kinney not looking like himself had made us mute. His elderly mother, by the casket, turned and refused to speak to Stan, the lover, who, as everyone knew, had given the blessing of the final kiss and closed up her son's eyes at the last.

The plaid-skirted Russian girl stopped and looked up something in a small book. I smiled as I went past. Her friend waited, nodding to me at the corner, at the crosswalk light I'd just missed because I was standing there gawking.

This happened during a time when I'd accumulated too much money in too many accounts—up north in one country and down south in another. The settlement that had come to me from the Burlington Northern Railroad was growing, but I barely kept track. I couldn't work up any interest in interest. There seemed to be nothing to do with it, or for it, or to it—as if I lived in the tropics and had a barn out back stacked high with logs for a woodstove.

The girls bent close to the book, searching out some mystifying English word, which was apparently not there. Pages turning fast in their fingers. *So lutely,* they said. They frowned at each other. Shrugged. Try *lutely,* said the one not holding the book.

After I'd taken the clothes to the church, I'd gone home for my furniture. Then the dishware. I'd planned a complete "re-outfitting"—that's the word that came to mind in those days. But coming home from the church and hearing my steps echo through the empty house, I was delighted—like someone shipwrecked in a new, uninhabited world. Through the drape-less windows, the light seemed a never-before-seen light.

I was still wearing my big clunky brown glasses. With them I could see details in the distance. No doctor had yet scowled into an X-ray of my eye, a lit negative I couldn't even see myself when he showed it to me and I stepped close: a woman staring hard at the blur that's made her world a blur.

Blanket. Books. Bed. I also kept the antiquated hi-fi system that played everything in a slowed-down tempo.

Nice suit, I'd whispered as the Russian girls turned up Third Avenue. They would probably put their scarves on their heads before they got home. But right then the scarves were tied around their necks. Gold and crimson and purple. Abso*lutely* lovely. The two girls brightening our blah Third Avenue for a few minutes that day.

It was a simple day of simple deeds. I hadn't yet been left half-blind. I hadn't yet written a large check to a wizened white-haired woman so that I could take over her dead son's cookware business and its thousand attendant worries. Everyone was still sad about the *Challenger*'s dead astronauts, a catastrophe forever blazing in the heavens with my own husband. I hadn't yet had to sue any doctors or dress in the dark or feel my way to the door. I had forty-eight books. A mattress on the floor. The fast music had a slower, sweeter cadence. I had a sky-blue blanket.

Retro Xmas

Lynette, age 21, 1978

Lynette had been running one second, and the next lay face down in the snow. "Oh," she called as she fell. "Oh." The fresh inch covering the church parking lot suddenly seemed a white sheet of deceit. She twisted to her side. Her left knee felt like a hubcap someone was pounding the dings out of.

"Think you broke anything?" a man's voice said.

She wiped a handful of snow from her cheek and looked up. A ruddy-faced man in a brown robe stood above her. He wielded a shepherd's crook, and for a second Lynette thought he might be about to bring it down on her shoulder.

"Who are you supposed to be?" she asked him as she began gathering up her sprawled limbs like an armload of dropped kindling. Both elbows felt far away and foreign.

"Tonight he's just plain old Joe," said a woman who suddenly appeared beside him. She was also in a robe, a long navy one. She passed the man a lit cigarette. Perhaps they were from a choir, Lynette thought, getting herself to a sitting position and patting around in the snow, groping for her glasses, which had flown off somewhere.

"She's got blood on her knee," Joe said in the pause after he'd inhaled and just before the smoke sailed back out.

Lynette's coat had fallen open, and when she looked at her knee, the pain there seemed to thicken. The red tip of Joe's cigarette was pointed right at it.

"Why would anyone be in shorts in the friggin' middle of December?" he asked and bent toward her, leaning on his crook.

"It's my uniform," Lynette said. "I've got to get to work. Do you guys know the time?"

"Can you even stand?" The woman held down a hand to her.

"It's going to be a long night if I can't," Lynette said and grabbed the hand.

Just then Joe aimed the crook toward her, hooking it under the arm she was using to push herself up. But the crook only jerked her arm out from under her, and Lynette fell back on her hip, pulling with her the blue-robed woman, who toppled forward to her knees.

"Hey!" Lynette shouted.

"You shithead, Eddie," the woman said, maneuvering back to her feet.

Joe, or Eddie, wrapped both hands around the crook as if to rein it in, as if it alone had perpetrated the misguided overture of aid.

Then, from across the parking lot came a high-pitched whine, like the cry of an old woman. Lynette squinted in that direction but saw only a blur of falling snow.

Joe leaned down, picked up Lynette's glasses, looked them over, and handed them to her. "You lucked out," he said, "they ain't broke."

The robed woman extended her hand again, and this time when Lynette took it, she managed to get to her feet. The knee had a siren of throb-throb-throb going off inside it. Beneath her coat, she ran her hands down her spine. There was no pain there. She put on her glasses and glanced over Holy Redeemer's red roof toward 29th Street, where she'd been headed. The lights of the businesses were slow to come into focus. However fine and straightened out her formerly scoliotic back was now, her vision was more crooked than ever.

"So that's a uniform?" Joe's gaze was fixed on her black shorts. Lynette's co-workers called them hot pants. They'd been all the rage three years earlier when Lynette was just starting college.

"Yeah." She jerked her coat closed and fumbled with its buttons. "Believe me, I don't like it either."

"Let me guess," the woman said. "That disco bar up the street. Retro something."

"Blast. Retro *Blast*." Lynette took two tentative steps and winced. She thought if she could just stop seeing herself still splattered there on the pavement, maybe her mind could override the pain, convince the rest of her that the fall hadn't happened. Or that it had happened so long ago it was no longer of consequence.

"Sometimes we hear their whoop-de-do way up here," Joe said.

Her vision slowly clearing, Lynette could make out—behind the robed couple—a flimsy plywood hut enveloped in tiny gold lights. Then she remembered. "So, you two are with that manger display?"

"You never heard of a live nativity?" Joe asked.

The woman laughed. "Semi-live," she said, "since we're half-froze out here." Her laugh revealed a black tooth, or perhaps a missing one, top right.

Joe stubbed out his cigarette with his boot, and Lynette saw that he had on black ski pants beneath the robe.

"Tonight's kind of it for us," said the woman. "They can't pay us enough to horse around for one more night in this snow."

"You're *paid* to do this?" Lynette asked. The snowflakes drifting down had gotten bigger.

"We're filling in for my brother and sister-in-law," the woman said. "They had a chance to go skiing up in Canada."

"Even though this is *their* stinking church," Joe said. "Marlene's relatives will pay people to do anything. They have a girl who cleans their toilets and some uptown kid who changes the art on their walls once a month."

The woman, Marlene, shrugged and rolled her eyes.

Behind them a stopped car honked, then revved and passed through the four-way intersection, over which the deserted little crèche seemed to preside like a roadside tollbooth.

"I've got to get moving," Lynette said, but when she took a step, she found that her knee had gone stiff. Great, she thought. How was she supposed to go off and dance now? How would she last until 2 A.M. in her wrought-iron disco cage?

"Wait." Joe was taking something from inside his robe. "You ought to have a swig of holiday cheer first." He uncapped a silver flask and passed it to her.

"The girl's got to get to work, Eddie," Marlene said. "She has an actual job." Then she turned to Lynette. "Go ahead, though, honey. It'll do you good." She smiled.

Lynette lifted the flask to her mouth, swallowed, and felt a warmth leak slowly into her chest. She closed her eyes and let it spread. The cage that waited for her at Retro Blast resembled a parrot's—papered on the bottom with dollar bills, money she intended to use to buy the last five classes that would buy her a diploma which would secure her a better job, maybe in a pretty town on the coast. This was 1978, a time when she still had plans like that, big plans. Everything added up to something else in an ongoing equation. But the diploma itself—as it turned out—would arrive in the mail with her name misspelled. *Linnet,* it would say. Like the bird. Years later, from beneath sweaters in a drawer, it would mock her: *Linnet, you flap real pretty. Give us a smile, Linnet.*

"Hey, where's the Virgin?" a boy yelled out the window of a Camaro that thundered through the intersection, his shout followed by another high whine from the plywood hut.

"There's no *baby* over there, right?" Lynette asked, realizing it was less a question than a statement of . . . what? Some moral imperative?

Joe turned sharply and gave the boy in the Camaro the finger. "Jerk-off," he called.

"Come back this way for a minute," Marlene said, taking the flask from Lynette. "We can put something on that knee, and I'll show you the baby."

As Lynette took another step, she felt a trickle of blood start down her shin. Surely Dr. Boss, the manager at the Blast, would forgive her lateness when he saw that knee.

Joe offered her the crook, but she shook her head. Between him and Marlene, Lynette limped toward the three-sided hut, which faced at an angle toward the intersection. Drivers from each direction could see into it, though just then there was nothing in there to see. With yellow straw heaped in the corners and its pulsing gold Christmas bulbs, the hut looked like a flashing caution light. Drivers honked. They slowed, stopped, then continued on.

"I've got to see a man about a horse," Joe said and stepped behind the hut. "Finally this damn robe is good for something."

From behind the plywood came the sound of a hard spray, like a spigot twisted on. Lynette glanced at the woman. They were standing to the side of the crèche, where the smell of the pungent vapor wafting off was unmistakable.

Marlene took a sip from the flask and passed it again to Lynette. "Come on inside," she said. "I know I've got a hankie in my purse."

Lynette blinked, adjusting her eyes to the twinkling lights, though unable to make out what, exactly, the fuzzy-faced doll in the manger was. Something swaddled in blue bunting.

Then the face moved. It had whiskers, and the whiskers twitched.

"*What?*" Lynette bent toward it, squinting.

It whined.

"Sit here, honey, and let me see that leg." Marlene squatted and began digging through a red vinyl purse she'd produced from under a stool.

Lynette stood staring down into the manger.

"Oh, him. That's just Marty." She patted the stool. "Come on. Sit."

"A dog?" Lynette said. "Is that a dog?" She sat down slowly.

"It's a little porker pig," Joe said, stepping inside the crèche and lifting the flask from Lynette's hands. "He's a potbellied one. The runt of his litter." Joe took a long sip.

Marlene held up a lace-edged handkerchief and snapped the purse closed. She took the flask from Joe, tipped it, and let a trickle seep into the cloth.

Lynette leaned toward the manger. The pig was on his side. His long pink snout had two little holes over a crisply downturned frown. His small front hooves lay atop the blue blanket that covered the rest of him. When he wheezed, his bristly whiskers quivered. He sounded like a kid with the croup.

"We used to have around ten of them," Joe said. "This one's the last, though. Some people eat them. We never did."

"No," Marlene said. "No way." She touched the top of the pig's head. "We had to bring Marty tonight," she said. "He's sick. He needs his pills."

"He's old." Joe looked down and sucked in his lower lip. "Heart trouble. His days are numbered."

Marlene pressed the damp hankie against Lynette's knee.

Lynette jerked. The burn sent bolts of yellow zigzagging across the insides of her closed eyelids.

"I'll bet that smarts," Joe said.

"Shut up, Ed, and pass her another swig."

The pig wheezed and let out a high, shrill wail. Lynette sipped as the woman dabbed. When she finally opened her eyes, she saw that her knee was freckled with specks of gravel. The bits seemed to be wedged inside a few raw crevices just below her kneecap. She handed Joe the flask and, taking a deep breath, used her fingernails like tweezers to pull out a pebble.

Marlene wrinkled her nose and blotted the hanky against the red crack where each stone had been.

They did this four more times, Lynette sighing and taking a sip after each dislodging. The pebbles plinked when they hit the vinyl purse by Mary's feet.

Joe lit another cigarette and gazed toward the cars now lined up behind the four stop signs. Illuminated by opposing headlights, each driver's face was smug and superior when it was his turn to go.

"Hear that? Listen," Joe said. "You'd think those fools up at Retro Blast needed that loud bass just to remind them they're not dead."

Lynette—her whole torso suffused with warmth now—nodded to him. To have made such an utterance at that moment seemed the reason Joe was standing there, his face serious, watchful.

Lynette looked up the street. There was a new dishwasher working there now, a sweet kid named Jack. He'd just bought a truck and had offered her a ride to work tonight. Why hadn't she said yes? And no doubt another girl was already subbing for her in the cage: another red-lipped lure on a line that dangled down into the school of open-mouthed men. Bottom-feeders, Lynette called them. They fed off detritus. The tedious music a current that slogged them along.

"I can get us more of that elixir if need be." Joe's voice seemed to drift in from a distance.

Marlene bent over the pig. "Porkie pie," she called him and stroked his snout. His tiny brown eyes watched her; he seemed calmer. Someone had taken the crèche—as if it were a thing inside a paperweight—and shaken it. But now, now all had settled. All was still, even the pig.

"I was expecting a doll," Lynette said. "Or maybe a Presto log." She pushed a few strands of hair off her forehead.

"They don't allow graven images at this church." Marlene's words emitted a piquant fog in the cold air. "Which, I guess, is why we're here. We're not graven, are we, Ed?" She smiled at him, her face blinking on and off: pale and gold, gold and pale.

Lynette pivoted on the stool and watched the cars: taking turns, but not happy about it. A driver glancing toward the crèche would have seen not one but two holy mothers bent over the child, while the poor stepfather sulked and smoked as if wondering when the Magi might appear. Where were the gifts?

A claxon sounded then—loud, demanding. Nine o'clock, Lynette realized, the hour of the shift change at the aluminum plant; she envisioned the plant's parking lot emptying and refilling like a sponge. She reached down and rubbed the pig's nose. It was cold and damp.

"He likes you," Marlene said. "And he doesn't like just anybody." She spread the dark robe over her legs.

"His poor old heart's ticking down to its last tock," Joe said.

The pig did indeed look as if he were dying, and Lynette sat up straighter, aware now that she was somehow prepared for just that—for a death right here in their midst, in the snow and the traffic and the hurt that kept her sitting there sipping from the flask whenever it came her way, which it did, right then, again.

"The girl can't go back out there." Joe turned to Marlene. "Tell her, Sugar. Tell her. She's had an accident. That's a bum knee."

Then Joe turned his attention again to the honking traffic and to the snow blowing lightly into their hut, which Lynette could plainly see was a good thing—yes, good—the hut, so that the hurrying travelers might pause, gaze toward them, and laugh a little laugh or feel a brief hiccup of happiness.

"She knows, Ed," Marlene said. "She's going to help me now. We're going to give Marty his pill."

One-Eyed and Halfway Home

Lynette, age 40, 1997

Blindness may be one way out of the two countries. Freezing to death could be another. I'm guessing there are many, really.

I doze, sightless, in my little gray car on a gravel lane—twenty yards from Canada, twenty yards from the U.S. From their squat white guardhouses, the two border guards stare at my car. Neither boy will let me pass. I can't see them, but I can hear their walkie-talkies click on and off. *Roger, she can just sit there a while. Roger that, yeah, till she gets her head on straight.*

The laser pulse had gone bad in my eye. In the recovery room, the nurse stood rattling her rosary. Dr. Goof in the doorway: trying but not able to make her stop. *Calamity,* she'd said, thinking, I suppose, I was deaf too.

I was asleep but dreaming myself awake and driving blind into Nelway and the border crossing there, where they knew me and usually waved me through. But not today. No sir. Not with these bandages on my eyes.

Shouldn't someone put her out of her misery? Was that what the nurse had said? To her rosary? To the doctor? All the patient (me) would have left—for all her time remaining on this earth—were her memories. Whatever the hell *those* were. The nurse was a white blur in the beige room. She wished, she said, it had turned out differently.

I had a great deal of cash—pretty blue bills in one pocket and faded green ones in another—but neither of the guard boys wanted it. *Have any smokes?* they asked.

I was a no-go, they said. *But I've driven this road a thousand times,* I told them. *I can absolutely feel it,* I said, *every curve. No worries,* I told them. *Those stop signs—I've got a good sense of them. And I'll stop—sure, just in time. Everything will be okay.*

The boys had to smoke for a while to think this over.

I don't want to blame my mother. That's my old way out of things. She'd been sure that Canada was the place to go since the surgery was so cheap up there, and if she paid for one eye, couldn't I pick up the tab for the other? Wouldn't that make a nice Christmas gift? Wasn't that a sweet little plan?

The patient would have a headache when she woke. And the kind thing to do would be to get that head on a stump and bring the ax down swiftly. Was this the doctor talking?

If it was spring, wasn't it time for me to be home? Didn't they expect me there? Out of the seventh century, there'd been a Homeric Hymn. Demeter, the plump earth, had a child who was lost. Terrible grief sung about in beautiful rhymes. Grieving so, Demeter withheld her gifts from the earth. Rivers froze, then the lakes and the oceans and the lands hither and yon. The glaciers rolled along.

The headache seems worse now. Is there something you could give me?
Something, yes, something, of course!

The doctor stuck his face into the hallway. *Girl,* he called. Or was it *Gail*? I was in a chair and had put my head back against the concrete wall. Gail, or girl, he told me, would make me comfortable. Tomorrow, after a slight alteration, I'd be as right as rain.

Why did this patient have this fever? The doctor put his big hand on my forehead, then jerked it away. *Yowzer,* he said, *that's a hot tamale.*

Over each white guardhouse, a flag flapped in the wind. I could hear them. The stars and stripes made a whooshing flap; the maple leaf was a whook-whook. Between them the gravel lane was full of potholes. No country owned it, so no country was responsible for fixing it. Under my white bandages, I saw the blind entering their own country. They held out their arms as if to embrace it. Their landscape was immense: rolling black plains, black hills, fast black rivers.

Galilee

Lynette, age 40, 1997

Marlene said Teddy liked to peel her black stockings down. She said he wouldn't do another thing until he'd twirled them neatly into two little coiled nests. She said his hands shook. Lynette had seen that. They shook all the time, especially when he talked, enunciating his words—like italics. Trembling italics, Lynette thought. Teddy had chewed his fingernails until only the red, raw slots of the nails were left: scarred crevasses. While Teddy coiled her stockings, Marlene said she sat quietly and watched snowflakes blow off patches of bank-bound river ice.

Teddy tried not to tickle her. He told Marlene he didn't want their lovemaking to be un-serious. His fingers, she'd mentioned to Lynette, felt like snow—cool, tapping and touching lightly, icing her thighs. And then his lips went there.

Lynette had been at Von's that November night when Marlene met Teddy, a man who once made his living on top of Brahma bulls. He still worked for the Interstate Rodeo Commission—in marketing now. Where first Teddy's left eye had been, and then for a time a shiny glass eye, now under a brown leather patch there was only the funnel the scalpels left. The bull that had gouged out Teddy's eye was still a mainstay of the rodeo. From the stands people cheered him. Never mind any man jostling on the bull's bony back. *Al-riiiight, Grenade!* the fans shouted, calling the bull by his rodeo name, although the cowboys knew him simply as the Bastard. Teddy didn't mind telling the story of the bull's horn going into his skull

107

and lifting him, like a fork spearing a steak, into the dusty air. He said he told it maybe five, six times a week. It was a true story, he said, the kind that sold rodeos to even the smallest, poorest towns out west.

And because he kept company with a few big-time promoters, he was sure that one of these days he'd figure a way for Marlene to meet Jane Fonda. Marlene had all of Jane's workout videos. "I could do the routines in my sleep," she'd told Lynette once.

"Maybe you do," Lynette said. "Maybe you do and you don't even know it."

Marlene had a plan. She thought if she were to meet Jane and if Jane were looking to make a new tape, Marlene would be the perfect assistant. She could stand in the background in her black leotard, gold stars blinking across her chest, and mimic Jane's every move. Then the viewers at home in their basements would see how easy it was, how painless. They'd see that they too could have Jane's body, as Marlene did— from pecs to abs to glutes. She was, Lynette guessed, only half-serious about the plan, and it had become a little joke, a little levity amidst the Chef's Pal cookware, between them.

"And why not?" Marlene said. "I'm a real person like all of them. Living proof of the magic of Jane's method."

"It's in the hopper," Teddy said. He'd stopped by the shop and purchased a melon baller. He claimed he had the rodeo's booking agent working on the Fonda plan. The next time the agent was in L.A., he'd call Jane up.

"Jane's good folk," Teddy told Marlene and Lynette. It turned out that Teddy had seen Jane, though they'd never exchanged words. In the Phouc Vinh Army Hospital, just days after almost all the shrapnel had been extracted from Teddy's chest, Jane had made a pass through his ward. She'd worn black leather pants and a red leather vest. *"Tight,"* Teddy said, his hands rising and falling, and his one eye's blue iris turned up bright in its socket. Then he smiled. Not a lot made Teddy smile, but Lynette saw that anything that did made Marlene look up at him and nod.

The one piece of shrapnel the doctors hadn't got still floated inside him—a foreign souvenir, a tiny relic that he knew could bob at any moment toward one of his heart valves. "And then *whammo!*" Teddy had told them, laughing and snapping two nubby fingers.

"Marlene's promiscuous," Lynette's mother said, a word Lynette wasn't sure pertained as well in 1997 as it had in 1957, when she'd been conceived.

Then Lynette heard herself say the same words to her mother that she'd said eleven years ago to Jack. "Marlene *is* how she is. You don't have to like her. She's *my* friend."

About the men in her life, Marlene had told Lynette that she considered herself more an escort than a mistress. More a loving companion than a companionable lover. She said none of the men wanted to love her in that thorough, penetrating way—the kind of love, she said, she used to be all about. Back when she was married to Eddie.

Eddie's name rarely came up, but when it did, Marlene usually pulled in her lips as if to stop them from trembling, as if to yank herself back from the edge of tears. In Lynette's fleeting memory of Marlene's husband Eddie, he stood outside a church, smoking in a snowfall. That was how Lynette had met him, met them both, years ago. They'd helped her up from a bad fall on the ice. Lynette wasn't yet married to Jack and Marlene not yet divorced from Eddie. The future and its oddly meandering, slippery, mud-rutted, and impossible-to-see-to-the-end-of-the-road still seemed to them a happy adventure. They put on their dark glasses and drove into it.

It had gone by fast—a lot of it in what she and Marlene called "mall time." "I'll meet you at six, mall time" meant they'd meet after work by the mall's kissing-frogs fountain. Marlene, who sold pipes and tobacco in a smoke shop there, had been the one to tell Lynette to chuck the crappy disco job and apply at a new little store that was just opening. The Chef's Pal. That was twelve years ago. Having begun as a stock person, then later a salesgirl, now Lynette was still a stock person and a sales-person, but also a bookkeeper, marketer, owner, and manager. And when the smoke shop had gone belly-up, Lynette, despite her mother's snide remarks, had offered Marlene a job.

"Eddie's moved on," Marlene told a man who had come into the Chef's Pal with his wife to buy a plastic colander. Hearing Marlene say that about Eddie, Lynette looked up from sorting the new stock of cookie cutters. Marlene had four colanders—silver, blue, yellow, and red—splayed out in her fingers like a huge hand of cards. She was smiling. She'd recently begun seeing Teddy, and they were having what she called "a fun old time."

The night Marlene and Teddy met was the night he'd just received his new eye. Lynette's Uncle Mel had driven him to the office of a famous "eye designer," a man who painted irises and pupils and even the little veiny red lines in the eyeball to match the client's.

"Actually this eye's quite a disappointment," Lynette had heard Teddy confess to a table of card players that night. "I half-thought I might be able to see *some*thing," he'd said. "I know them doctors said 'no way,' but still, you think things. You can't help it."

They were all assembled at Von's, where another of Lynette's uncles, Carl, had gotten Marlene a second job serving drinks. This was last November, when the smoke shop at the mall had just begun floundering and Marlene's hours were cut back.

"These cards are getting soggy." Carl scooped them up and handed them to Lynette. "Honey, look in back and see can you find us a dry deck." Her Uncle Carl was trying to make some winnings off a boy named Chad who'd won $2,200 bronc-riding that afternoon and was now buying rounds and tipping big. Lynette had guessed that by the end of the evening, he'd barely have bus fare back to Ellensburg. But she'd been wrong about that.

When she handed Carl the new cards, sealed in cellophane, he glanced at her and said that if she had any sense at all, she'd head home later with a "real champeen," and he nodded to Chad. The boy looked away. It was clear to her he was afraid of her. He could hang on to a half-wild horse one-handed, but Lynette was a breed apart. A horse of another color. He had the sort of ears people used to call cauliflower. He had scrapes on his arm, bruises on his neck. He was barely out of his twenties. But still Lynette offered him a smile as she helped Marlene clear away empty glasses.

Looming up like a blue jewel in the smoky room, Teddy's new eye seemed to watch them, following them to the bar and back. Teddy was telling the story of the Bastard. He was at the part where the horn that sticks him is "two foot long." His hands with their wild jacks and deuces fluttered in the air.

"This thing itches," Teddy said as his money piled up. His good eye gave Marlene a wink. He pawed at the glass eye. He was, surprisingly, the one who was winning. Thinking about it now, that was, Lynette guessed, the beginning of his luck.

Around the table the hands folded one by one. "It itches bad," Teddy said as he raked in more money and, in practically the same motion, lifted one hand to his face and took out the eye. "I'm giving this thing a rest." He plunked it in his empty shot glass, where it stared through the thin amber film into the bottom of the table. Then he put his head back and set an ice cube in the pit where the eye had been. "Ah. Much better."

"Are you in or out?" Uncle Carl asked him.

Teddy, his head still tilted back, just waved his hands.

"That guy's a riot," Marlene said to Lynette in the kitchen.

The eye was never seen after that. Her Uncle Mel believed that Von might have accidentally thrown it out with the dregs of drinks long after Marlene and Lynette had gone home and left the guys to what was left of two bottles of Jack. Her Uncle Carl thought that maybe it had been pocketed by someone else at the table as a cruel joke, or out of spite about Teddy's winnings. At any rate, by the time the men stood up to leave, they'd forgotten themselves too much to remember such a thing as an eye.

"Useless damn piece of glass anyhow," Teddy said a couple weeks later. And that was all he'd ever said about the lost eye. The only thing the doctors at the VA Hospital would tell him was, sorry, that was all he got, that was the one and only eye the government would shell out for.

Early December. The Christmas rush was upon them at the Chef's Pal, and Lynette was glad to have Marlene's help.

"She's a far better salesperson than I am," Lynette told her mother. "She's got a natural way with people. They take to her right away."

"Such was sort of my point," her mother said, and Lynette realized she'd left herself wide open for that.

Through December, Marlene had grown fond of Teddy. *Fond.* That was her word. She said they made a kind of love. Not the kind she'd ever whisper *please* for, putting her lips on his ear or her hand on the zipper of his jeans. She said lately she'd come to want less and was learning to like better what was around to like. Teddy ran his cool, trembling hands all over her. She said he never took his jeans off, or his shirt. He moaned, though, when she combed her fingers across his scalp.

And he liked to watch her sweating in her workout routines. He claimed it was a major turn-on. He told her she had a capacity to arouse him without even trying. Sometimes he'd sit in a dark corner of her den, and his hand would go into his pants. He thought she didn't see, but she did. That was the way he wanted it. Jane's voice was soothing to them both. "Squeeze those glutes," Jane would say. "Yeah, baby," Teddy would answer back. Marlene would be on the floor huffing and puffing, her legs flailing.

Lynette had been only slightly more surprised than Marlene was when in early January Teddy had said he wondered whether Marlene would mind sharing her "kind and generous affections" with his old friend Winstead Van Epp.

"It's weird, isn't it?" Marlene asked Lynette in Von's restroom. Teddy was waiting just outside. "What do you think? *Too* weird?"

"Well, what do *you* think?" Lynette answered. They were running their hands together under icy water at the same sink, watching each other's eyes in the mirror. Marlene's were bright, amber with green flecks. Her own, she saw, seemed far away, a dim brown under the heavy glasses.

"I'm leaning in the direction of yes."

Lynette grabbed a towel. She'd met Winstead. They both had. A pal of Teddy's from the VA Hospital, he'd played cards a few times at Von's. "Just so you know, Marlene," Lynette said, "Winstead's missing a few screws. Just so you know that."

Marlene nodded into the mirror. Clearly she knew. She seemed to be considering the breadth of her benevolence.

Back at the table, Teddy seemed to understand what had transpired in the ladies' room. He stood up and held out Marlene's chair, then Lynette's. "I have to tell you frankly," he said to Lynette, "I'm not entirely releasing her from my love. This ain't the end of anything."

Watching them together, Lynette felt sure she knew far less about love's difficulties than Marlene did. But she was learning. Marlene offered advice. She'd weathered the beginning, middle, and ending of that fifteen-year marriage to Eddie. She said she was trying to find direction, and the last Sunday of June she'd called and suggested that they put on their flowered skirts and white sandals and go sit for a while in church.

"What church?" Lynette said.

"You pick," Marlene said. "I'm not choosy. So long as there's a choir."

They found themselves at the little church outside of which they'd met years ago, and they laughed remembering the snowy night, the cut on Lynette's knee, where there wasn't even a scar now.

"I hadn't even met Jack yet, I don't think," Lynette said, looking around in the parking lot, trying to remember the time sequence. She saw herself working in the wretched disco bar, wearing the ridiculous black hot pants, flirting with Jack in the kitchen. Lynette and Jack. They seemed to have existed not so much in an earlier life but in an altogether other one.

"You need to shed those widow weeds, dearie," Marlene said. "You were married to him a decade ago."

Lynette turned to her as Marlene swung open the church door. Suddenly there was organ music. Someone stuck a program in her hand.

They sat on a pew in back. Lynette had to smile when the oval trays with grape juice and bread cubes came around. She recalled how as a girl she'd sucked on the tiny squares of Wonder Bread until they dissolved like mints in her mouth. "Take, eat. This is my body," the minister had repeated. The bread's slow dissolve had intrigued her as a girl, but now, as an adult, she felt greedy. She'd had no breakfast. She took a half-dozen cubes, palming them as the tray went past.

Lynette's dismissal of the rodeo boy Chad nagged at her. It seemed evidence of what she worried might be her unloving nature—an uncharitable self. Chad was a shy, well-intentioned kid. Over his eyes that had watched her that night were eyebrows frozen into two relentless question marks. He'd told her he was taking college classes "now and then" and hoped to go into banking. Once or twice Lynette had tried to imagine an embrace with him, visualizing her face and lips nearing those large ears. Would she, could she, kiss them? And smiling at her last week from across five empty tables, still believing her to be a waitress there, he'd asked her, simply and quietly, when would her shift be over. *Never* was what she'd wanted to say, although she'd only shrugged and slipped out the back door. And now it occurred to her that the huge ears had heard anyway—heard way down into the sordid depths of her cruelty, into her *No-way-in-hell* and into an increasingly deafening *Never. This shift end? Never. Never.*

In church the minister was talking about the hungry crowd on the shores of Galilee, and Lynette sucked the bread cubes, one by one, half-dozing and imagining what would happen after the purple-robed man on the cross in the stained-glass window slipped down: the crosshatching of his flesh with knives . . . so that later it could be handed out, piece by piece, to the hungry ones. Like her. Or to the weeping ones, like Marlene, who dabbed at her eyes just then and chewed the sweet white bread of the body.

Marlene had come up with an idea that Lynette thought was nutty. A weekend cooking class of "rodeo food." She'd broached this in early February, and Lynette thought, Ah, only three months here, and already the gal's putting new plans into motion.

"Rodeo food," Lynette said. "Now, just what is that?"

"It's everyone's favorite—you know, chili, barbequed ribs, all sorts of biscuits and cornbread and maybe fritters."

"Ugh," Lynette said. "Who can't make that?"

"People are always trading recipes for that sort of stuff. For each class, we could offer a meal menu with a very special spin. Say chili with chocolate in it. Not everyone knows about that."

"Double ugh."

Marlene tipped her head and shook it. "I knew you'd say that, Lynnie."

But Lynette had posted a sign-up sheet—just to see, she said, if it drew any takers. And of course it did—a good-sized group, and, as Marlene had promised too, an easy prep and cleanup. For each class they'd featured a different pricey piece of cookware—an electric rotisserie, a bronze miniature biscuit pan. And yes, Lynette had to admit, it had been good for business.

And Marlene had been right too about the new man, Winstead Van Epp, although he was, Marlene said, initially difficult to love. His head was perfectly bald on top; over his ears was a shag of white hair—whether blond or old-timer white, no one, not even Winstead himself, was sure. When Winstead talked, he shouted.

Marlene said she'd had to search deep down to find a teensy ember of interest she could blow on, that she could get glowing. She said she kept having to tell Winstead to be quiet. "Whisper," she'd told him that first time in her bed, but he couldn't. He didn't know how. He'd lain back, rigid as a plank, on the mattress, but he'd let her touch him everywhere. He was not aroused—not exactly. But he was interested. Once, after a couple months, he'd cried. She'd brushed her breasts across his face, and there'd been tears to meet them.

As they'd left the church that day last summer, Marlene had suggested that Lynette might be using Jack's death as an excuse for not letting a man get close to her again. And Lynette had been thinking about this. Was she living now as if all routes into her deepest feelings had been seared with a hot iron? Her dark little heart sat tight with puckered skin all around it. She was a thirty-nine-year-old widow. Had she become enamored of her own pain? When it hurt, did she want it to hurt more? After the train had crashed eleven years ago into and through her husband's truck, she'd wept when the railroad money came. She'd wept when the insurance money came. Checks drifted in, and she wept longer, harder, louder. She sat in her own sadness like a plump toad in a murky pond.

On the phone to Marlene last night, Winstead had shouted, "Marlene, if you want to fly down to L.A., the trip's on me. I got frequent flyer miles up the wazoo. And they're yours. Just say the word." Even from across the store, Lynette had been able to hear him as Marlene held the phone out from her ear. She shook her head. "*Kee-rist*," she mouthed into the air.

At home in his den, Winstead liked them to watch Jane together. But only watch. "You make me exhausted, sweetie," he'd boom to Marlene. "Please, can you stop all that jumping? My blood pressure's spiking off the charts." They'd sit on his sofa and turn the sound up high the way he liked. Marlene said she had to just imagine herself doing the steps, twirling and kicking her knees up. She'd gained ten pounds. And the recent taste "sampling" of rodeo food hadn't helped. "But," she said, "I am exceptionally good at Jane's routines in my mind."

When Marlene hung up, she told Lynette how lately she felt that when she came to Winstead and pressed herself around him, it was like touching a corpse—her flesh brushing up and down him as one might use a cloth to wash the dead. She said sometimes when she thought that way, there'd be tears on her own face.

In April a guy named Rodney crept into the mix—crept right up to the table at Von's and said he'd take whatever sort of love Marlene had left over. She needn't go to much trouble. He stood by the table, the one at which Lynette had stopped for a glass of wine, the one at which Teddy usually dropped

Marlene off for Winstead to pick up. The men's paths crossed like that, like old horses on a familiar path. Teddy usually shook Winstead's hand when Winstead and Marlene stood to leave.

That night Winstead glanced up and spoke calmly, not loudly, to Rodney. "It's up to her," he said. "Entirely up to her."

"Ditto what he just said." Teddy nodded to Winstead and then to Rodney.

A few minutes after that, Rodney was speaking to Marlene by the coat rack, and Lynette, putting on her scarf, heard him say again that he wouldn't ask for much.

"I don't think I possibly could," Marlene said.

Rodney put his fingers to his throat, where there was a dark shadow under his skin. He pressed on the shadow and his voice came out—high-pitched, slow, the bronchial wind pushing it. "I'm a friend of Winstead's. I know Teddy. We all three did time in the VA."

Lynette hurried, trying to get past the coats.

From across the restaurant, Winstead and Teddy nodded to Rodney, solemn and doleful. Then Teddy caught Lynette's eye. He shrugged. He wore a black patch now on the eye. His hands trembled as he stood and set his Stetson on his head.

In the parking lot, Lynette saw Chad sitting in his truck. He rolled down his window when he saw her. "How about I take you out for a steak?" he said. He tipped his head.

"Oh, no thanks, I just ate," she told him, which was a lie. Then she walked by him and got in her car. In the rearview mirror she watched Chad back up and speed out of Von's with a squeal onto the rain-slick street.

On the way home, Lynette pulled over and sat in the downpour and berated herself. Had she no capacity? Had she emptied herself of her last shred of humanity?

She thought of Marlene swabbing shelves, laughing, saying she guessed there were many degrees of closeness to have with men, and although right now none of them seemed exactly what she wanted, none was awful either.

"It's just flesh," Marlene had said. "It's just packages of flesh and bone going along together for a time. It's not such a big deal."

"I don't know," Lynette said. "I'm not sure. It's about what's passing through, though, too. Isn't it? *Isn't* it? And that could be a lot."

One day in early May, Marlene drove Lynette and Rodney to the Tekoa Rodeo. Lately Lynette had come to depend heavily on Marlene—to take care of things at the store, and to drive her places—since the Lasik surgery she'd had last month up in Canada hadn't gone well. Now her left eye saw everything tipped sideways, and it would—when she could work up the energy and the nerve—have to be redone.

When the three of them got out of the car, they heard Teddy's voice. He was speaking into a microphone from a booth over the bleachers. He was leading the Pledge of Allegiance.

They waited, surveying the crowd. Having left her cousin Jessie to take care of everything by herself at the Chef's Pal, Lynette worried about what could go wrong. What druggie friends might stop by? The cash. The unopened inventory.

"Anywhere you want to sit," Rodney kept saying to Marlene and Lynette, touching his throat, and Lynette saw Marlene reach down and take his hand. No doubt, Lynette thought, only an hour ago Marlene had sat naked in his lap.

It was a cool day, and half the bleachers were in the sun and half in the shade. "I'll sit anywhere," Lynette said. "It doesn't matter."

"You decide," Marlene said to Rodney.

He stopped, dropped her hand, and stared from her to Lynette.

"It's your life too," Marlene told him suddenly.

Rodney blinked into the sun. Then he put on his dark glasses and nodded to the sunny side.

About Rodney, Marlene will only say it's going to be a long, slow climb back up into life in the now. He's years behind. And he's writing a book about the time he never quite got through, though he's still polishing, after all these years, the same twenty pages of chapter one. In those pages, three men, boys really, lie on a beach by the South China Sea. They swim and work on their tans. They tell stories of big combines in the wheat fields back home, the dust and heat and terrible insects. Overhead a helicopter gunship roars by, the soldiers inside it leaning out, spraying ammunition into the water at some big fish, or dolphins maybe. Then the chopper, still spraying bullets, banks into a turn, and by the time the boys on the beach see it, it's too late for them to run for cover. "Ooow!" screams the boy in the middle, brushing at his chest with both hands. They all three stand up. The one to the left, who is Rodney, tries to pick away a pebble that's blown into his throat. His fingers come away sticky. *Tacky* is what he writes in his book.

The three of them see the helicopter rattle off. The one in the middle keeps brushing at his chest. Then he sinks to his knees on the sand. The boy on the right bends over him. "Get up!" he shouts. "Rod, help me get him up." Then the middle boy's eyes flutter closed; his head knocks back on his white towel.

The sand is dotted with blood. In chapter one, the sun is hot and the three boys have sunburns on their shins and knees. They'd been worried they'd have a rough night sleeping. As the chapter ends, Rodney is helicoptered to Saigon, the man in the middle dies right there on the beach, and the third man walks away and lies alone in his hot tent that night, tossing and turning and scratching at his sunburned legs.

Lynette had read the pages and encouraged Rodney. "It's great," she told him, "keep going."

"Yeah?" Rodney smiled. Then he flipped to page twelve and circled a word. "I'm still not sure about *flutter,*" he said. He'd typed on the top right side of every page: *Another Day, Another Death. Chapter One by Rodney S. Judson.*

"Start chapter two," she said. "This one's good. Let's see the next."

Rodney pushed at his throat. "It's slow goin', Lynette."

"What about all that time in the hospital?" she asked.

"Boring," he said, forgetting to press on the voice box so that the word came out as a garbled fuzz of sound, which she somehow still understood.

In the sunny bleachers, Marlene, Rodney, and Lynette watched the cowboys throw calves to the ground. The rope went around the front hooves, then the back. "It's a special sort of rope," Lynette explained to Rodney, "plastic-coated," although she could barely see it. She leaned toward him. She felt herself nearing the end of loving her own loneliness.

When the Grenade, a.k.a. the Bastard, hurled himself out of the chute with a young red-headed boy on his back, no one was yelling louder than Teddy up in the announcer's booth. "Ya-hoo," he squealed over the mike, which echoed and twanged. The Bastard's huge white horns flashed in the sun, and Lynette leaned forward, squinting to see the big head, trying to catch a glimpse of his eyes, to see if there was still murder in them. He quickly tossed the boy off his back.

"Not bad for an animal that's ten years old," Teddy said over the microphone. "That's sixty in bull years." The young cowboy kept searching for his hat in the manure-strewn ring as the bull ran by, and "Look, you two," Marlene said, "that's the bull that took Teddy's eye."

Lynette shaded her eyes with her hand, and Rodney leaned forward, his wheezing breath in her ear. Swishing its tail, the Bastard ran past, headed for the paddock gate as if he knew that his work for the day was done.

Rodney and Marlene had turned their attention back to the cowboy, who still hadn't found his hat. Of course not! Lynette thought. A clown had stolen it; this the crowd had seen at the exact moment the cowboy had gone sailing through the air. The clown had rushed across the ring, snatched up the hat, and was wearing it now, proudly, as if it were his.

"Oh my god," Rodney said perfectly, like a man whose voice was his own, not some box's. "That's Winstead. Look, girls, that clown is Winstead."

He was right. In the ring, Winstead flung his arms like a raving lunatic. No way he was giving the red-headed boy his hat back, and finally the boy just shrugged and walked away, his chaps rustling. Winstead tipped the hat to the crowd.

"Let's hear it for our newest member of the West One Rodeo family," Teddy said, "Winstead the Clown."

The applause was mild. Winstead bowed deeply from the waist. He wore huge clown ears so the hat sat amazingly high on his head.

Rodney clapped with great gusto. The sun grew even warmer. Marlene unbuttoned the two top pearly snaps of her western shirt and rolled up the sleeves. Then Lynette did the same. Marlene had flab now on her upper arms. Pale flab. It was skin that had, as yet, never been touched by the sun. The Jane Fonda workout she did, with Rodney watching, involved a de-suiting of her black spandex. Rodney tapped his feet to keep time as she pulled herself loose from the suit. Then she was on her hands and knees, kicking out her legs in back, and Rodney would get down on the floor to watch. "Marlene, Marlene," he'd murmur, touching his throat. "Now this is real video. Forget Jane. Let's pool our dough and make some tapes of our own."

Marlene said she only laughed and rubbed his shoulders. "It's just for you," she'd whisper, "just for you." She said she knew she was too chubby now. Jane would scoff. But no matter. She said she'd grown accustomed. She liked what she had. The little tire of flesh around her middle, the jiggling flab under her arms—she said it was fine.

And "Don't worry, Lynnie," she'd said about Chad. "He's not quite ready for a grown woman anyway, although you— you're not so grown you can't handle *him*." Lynette didn't entirely get it, but she sensed it was a thing that could one day be gotten.

The Tekoa Rodeo was the last one of the season. The wild ponies bucked and threw off their weights of men and boys. Everyone applauded the tumbles. *Ooo*, they cheered when the bodies flew high in the air. The higher the bodies went, the louder and longer the ooohing. At intermission the girls' drill team, in pink lamé blouses flashing with rhinestones, rode their horses into the ring. The girls carried flags from the western states, and largest and flapping out in front was the Stars and Stripes. Weaving in and out around each other, the horses made patterns. "Land of the pilgrims' pride," Rodney sang off-key through his aluminum box. There were tears in his eyes. Then in Marlene's. Then in Lynette's.

The drill team horses bucked and whinnied, and Lynette had the idea right then that everything might keep on in this way from here to forever. Each man leading to another. And yes, she thought, what's inside us may be meant to multiply like the loaves and fishes by the water. Or perhaps we *were* that water, salty and wide. The more that falls into us, the more we ripple out.

Getting Aunt Bette Dressed

Jessie, age 39, and Lynette, age 41, 1998

The younger cousin thinks the pink blouse insipid. The older one's hands tremble, lowering it over their great-aunt's head. Where are the shoulders? Jessie, help me find an arm. Someone in the hallway hums—as if that might hurry the women along.

They hurry. There's to be a high tea, and also delicate pastries in the newly restored turn-of-the-century downtown hotel. In the banquet room's stained-glass windows, stags, ducks, and pheasants are chased by hounds. A woman in an alcove strums a harp.

The great-aunt is a hook the pale blue sweater keeps slipping off. It's some joke her grand-nieces don't get. A third safety pin does the trick.

The older cousin stops and stares. The paper-thin skin over the aunt's hands appears to be embossed with runes. The younger cousin curses pantyhose, the already waning light, and what's with this weather, she says. Is it—jeez, Lynnie, yes, that's snow.

Misbuttoned buttons. Laughter and a gift bottle of wine it's absolutely time to open. The younger cousin finds the corkscrew. The other asks: The navy shoes or the gray ones? A pinker lipstick? No, the darker rouge.

_____

Night's begun its creep through the steady dusk of the body as the cousins press it forward, press it back. The old hotel withdrawing now from the young women's minds—the breaths of its barely breathing gargoyles swirl in the frigid air.

The semi-dressed one wears a black stole atop the blue sweater over the pink blouse over the white slip that covers the caved-in flesh where a breast once rose. The cousins set a tiny black pillbox hat atop the head. Surely the netting coming down over the eyes will be good, yes, all right. Aren't the leaf petals in the lace latticework lovely?

All right. Okay. None of the three women has the slightest inkling this'll be the last time they're all together. Out the window, car lights distill to dots in the darkening distance.

Then there's the auntie's grin that always frightened Great-Uncle Floyd and that now makes the moon slip out so early—so brazenly—from behind a cloud.

Twenty fingers pin twelve loose white hairs under the hat. A blue rhinestone brooch. Checking the time on the gold watch. Checking the necklace chain and the clasp, which the cousins have to trade eyeglasses to see.

Quite fine. Quite good.

But all activity ceasing when the Kool-Aid cart appears at the door: The quiet dignity of squat white cups. The solemnity of the cup-bearer nurse, and a shimmering crimson in a ritual that warrants Latin.

The tent of clothes rising and falling back. Sips all around of the sweet drink. Good. Quite good. A fresh fire under old kindling. What's begun to live, happily, at the end's beginning.

The older cousin saying somewhere there are gloves. The younger saying she might just go sneak a smoke in that light outside that she thinks is the color of iron. Both agreeing that only the flowered green-and-gold skirt fits around the old one's waist now. Fine, okay.

As the drink cart shimmies down the hall, a fresh hymn starts up. The cousins hum, the hurry gone out of them. And the impossible labor in here, as if the ancient body's invented more parts of itself, which spring forth to be clothed. Where are the bracelets of charms? The clean lace hanky?

The one smoking on the balcony about to disappear into her own blue smoke rings, and the one inside about to be the gluer of ancient bones, and nobody knowing any of this yet. Nobody even guessing.

The dressed one frowns. Where is her pocketbook? Nobody knows. Will she never be ready? At this hour she will surely need her skates. The god-awful too-tight tan ones, she says. It's the only way, she pleads, this late, to get to town on time across the icy river.

Never the Face

Lynette, age 42, 1999

After the laser beam's snafu with my right eyeball, everything had to come in close or I couldn't see it. February took too long and kept too quiet, and I sensed I might have to get hold of a bird—somehow—in order to glimpse its feathers, see the color and sheen. I practically had to take road signs, for Christ's sake, in my arms to read them.

Now I was jogging on a Montana dirt road east of Malta, no longer sure where I was, and so far from that *something*, I was sure I must be seeing it wrong. A bright purple-roofed house was walking—wobbling, really—toward me on feet in blue sneakers. That couldn't be right. The house took tiny steps, then paused like an animal that's just seen a predator . . . who could be, I realized suddenly, me.

My so-called sight was quasi-sight. I swore at it under my breath.

The house lurched another few steps in my direction and stopped. I squinted and slowed, slipping off my headphones. I thought I heard laughter from one of the house's upstairs rooms. Were those eyes and a nose in the attic window? Why couldn't the house pick a spot and sit still? It seemed to be taunting me, making me stand on the side of a road and call myself a shit-eyed idiot. Now the tiny walking house was making me question every clear sight I *thought* I'd had all day. Hadn't I seen a red-tailed hawk shoot down into a field of dirt clods and scuffle back up with a rodent wriggling in its claws?

I blinked. I'd been so sure, but maybe I'd been cocky. And now I was cockeyed again, piss-blind. Now nothing that came into view could be trusted.

A house comes walking toward a person. Does it expect a greeting?

I stood my ground. I was not afraid of a house wearing blue sneakers.

Then the house set itself down. Of this I was almost sure. Gone were its two little feet. The house was half my height, a plastic playhouse. These were guesses, maybes. The way *maybe* I'd recognize white teeth coming at me down a sidewalk, but not the face, never the face. Until it was quite *on* me. A wink—I could never get one close enough, or I'd get one too close, and by then it'd be gone. Back in January I'd had to sit so close to the Super Bowl, I could lick the players' faces on the screen.

Now as I stood in the road watching, a child—I *think*—opened the front door of the miniature house and stepped out, ducking under the doorway. She carried a small red hammer. She was wearing those blue sneakers. She turned and looked back at the house as if she'd just discarded a cocoon. Right then I would not have been surprised if she'd unfolded wings. But no.

She tapped at the roof that came up as high as her shoulder, a lovely roof the color of concord grapes. Then she turned to me. "You can't come in our yard," she said.

"I'm not," I said. "I'm only going by."

She crossed her arms over her chest. She had short dark hair in what we used to call a pixie cut.

"Cool house," I said. "Who lives there?"

She frowned and sighed deeply. She was forming a thought that clearly took some effort. "A lot of people. A very lot."

I realized then that I was passing the old Otto Lundstrum ranch. That would make this child some sort of cousin to me—a fourth or fifth, or maybe a third time removed. Only my Great-Aunt Bette would know. Only she was capable of deciphering the family-tree charts, and then I recalled that Aunt Bette was dead. She was herself among the tree's out-of-control branches that now no one knew how to prune or prop up. And this girl, this cousin, was somewhere amid all those stunted small twigs, but who, anymore, could say where?

Duh. She is right here, Lynnie, I said to myself. She was tapping a red hammer on a purple roof. No doubt she would soon put in hedges and flowers and have herself some babies to live up in the rooms with the orange and pink shutters. Tomorrow she would serve tea to foreign dignitaries. She was a Lundstrum.

She was of them, and I was of them, and they were the West once. They'd even tried to plant apple trees. These silly people. My kin. They'd been so sure, had that strong an inkling of Eden. They thought if they weren't exactly *in* it, they'd at least brushed up against it. I was from all that too. I'd walked on the back side of Brown Ridge among those shriveled apple trees that still produced their shriveled apples.

I began running again down the road. Once, glancing back, I saw the girl closing up the window shutters. She did this in a big hurry as if she'd seen signs, as if she knew a storm was coming. Against the dry beige field grasses, the girl's house was a shock of bright colors. I picked up my speed, humming to an oldie in my headphones, thinking such a sweet little house did indeed deserve such a stern proprietor so that no one would come by and walk off with it.

I worried as I ran. From the months of bringing so many things in so close, I worried that I'd crammed too much into too tight a space. And there I sat, a fat old minotaur, boring myself farther into the labyrinth's center, while perhaps a handsome gentleman began unspooling a thread . . . deeper and deeper . . . into, around, and through all this friggin' stuff, these obstacles pressing in.

He'd never find me. I could hardly find me. Everything was crowded in close. I could hardly move. I could barely breathe. Apparently I'd dragged a lake in here, and now—now I must go and get a mountain.

Boneland

Lynette, age 48, 2005

Oblivion

Thanks to the map Steve had drawn for me, I found the high school in Bozeman easily, but as soon as I stepped inside, I knew I'd entered by a wrong door. I walked down a hallway of classrooms. The Bach concert, Steve had said, was an afternoon "assembly" to which the public was invited. But glancing around, I suspected that the school's staff may have regretted its open-door hospitality.

The babies the high school girls had been carrying around were broken. Broken open. A thick white dust from the babies' insides had flown everywhere.

It was still flying.

The hallway was slick with it. White-speckled lockers and trophy cases. "We've killed our babies," a girl said as I passed her. She dangled an empty flour sack on her index finger. *Gold Medal*, it read, and I saw that a face—a goatee and cat whiskers—had been drawn on the sack in black Magic Marker.

Evidently the girls thought the bags of flour as dead babies hilarious. The girls watched me go by, their mouths and eyes eerily pink against their ghost-white faces.

If I could find my way through all this white, Steve would be waiting. I could feel him waiting—his face, his luminous blue eyes—like air above water under which I'd been holding my breath for an impossibly long time.

It was the third week of August, the first week of school. I walked past three teachers, Steve's colleagues, I thought— also white-splotched—standing with their arms crossed over their chests outside a classroom. They barely stopped scowling when I paused and asked directions. Then all three pointed me down the floured corridor.

This crush I had, this small, tight bud of the remote possibility of love, was leading me forward—this crush on someone who hadn't yet, as my Uncle Mel cautioned me, "gotten himself unmarried."

Yet. That was the word I repeated silently as I added my little sandal prints to the helter-skelter of prints down the long hallway. I felt I was headed straight for oblivion. I had to trust that however out of hand things had gotten here in the high school, the visiting string quartet from Fargo would still perform today, and that Steve's son Luke, a sophomore, whom I hadn't met, would still perform with them, a clarinet solo. An honor.

"My baby was way bad," a blonde girl up the hall called— to me or to the cheerleader I'd just passed, I wasn't sure. Then "Careful," she said, nodding at my feet.

Trudging through the white dust, my heart pounding, I doubted I'd ever return unscathed to what I was now thinking of as the Normal State. Washington. My normal state. These last three weeks in Montana had slogged by like three months. Back in the normal state, I kept thinking, people don't sit up past midnight gluing together the fossilized bones of some unidentified sauropod. Back in the normal state, houses have televisions. There are grocery markets with assorted lettuces, not just iceberg. Espresso stands and nail salons. Fitness clubs, video stores. A person didn't have to drive a hundred miles to hear Bach. Back in the normal state, I could get up in the morning and unlock my kitchenware shop in the mall and watch the world enter. I could take the world's money and send the world away again with something shiny and stainless steel.

Slamming locker doors, the girls sent clouds of flour swirling around me. I walked past a slashed-open flour bag on the floor—a pink baby bonnet askew on its half-full end.

Uncle Mel hadn't wanted me to leave the ranch to drive down here to Bozeman, where any minute now his old friend's son Steve Severson, Jr., would touch my arm, or take my hand. But I'd gotten in my car anyway, cranked up the AC, and driven out of the driveway, watching my uncle's frowning face, perfectly framed in my rearview, and then his back as he turned and walked toward the wheat field.

I worried he'd have a heart attack out there, down on his knees with the hand trowels, digging, without me, in the hot sun. And if he did end up prone in the freshly dug dirt, his eyes bulging, staring whitely at the enormous sky, it would be my fault. I knew that too. Clearly it was already my fault that Uncle Mel hadn't quit this foolishness and gone home to Spokane. To Aunt Dot. To the Normal State.

What Was He Thinking?

Whatever it was, god help me, apparently I was starting to get it.

All that he was unearthing up there in Malta made both of us blink hard in the blinding August sunlight, and it kept us awake at night too—fitful and wondering, and frankly a little stunned—in our separate sweltering upstairs rooms of the old Lundstrum family home.

In the high school hallway I had to touch the lockers for balance. My brown sandals had gone white. So had my toes, even my ankles.

Behind me the girls were shouting:

"That was the ugliest baby on the planet."

"Your baby's not dead yet. Finish him off."

"A real baby cries. A real baby goes, 'Ow, ow, ow.'"

I was nearing two big oak doors that I believed would open and release me into beautiful music and a man's fingers brushing my arm. I'd driven a hundred miles in a hundred minutes for that. But first, first I had to take these last few whiter and then whiter steps.

Back in the Normal State

Aunt Dot had told us she'd bent down, picked up a gold maple leaf, and found a miniature village beneath. There were domes, she said. Temples and mosques. Spiraled turrets, and the traffic of oxcarts on narrow pebbled streets. She guessed that the leaf had been a sort of awning for the whole village, and now that awning was gone.

And that, Dot said, was what she felt bad about. The village. It began growing too warm too fast—as if the fat old sun had pulled the distant strung-out planet up close for inspection.

My mother, hearing all this, looked at me and rolled her eyes. She was past caring whether Dot saw those looks.

This had transpired a few days before I packed a bag and headed out here to north-central Montana.

"After that maple leaf blew away," Dot went on, turning in her chair and glancing out the kitchen window, "I saw things I know I shouldn't have been privy to." She looked at me. "So why *was* I?"

I took a breath, then shook my head slowly.

"Lynnie, I felt like a giantess, a disrupter of a small, peaceful community."

I lifted an apricot from a bowl and bit into it. No doubt I'd be asked later what I thought we should do about Aunt Dot.

But right then, as after most of these stories, Dot suddenly smiled and said the usual: "It's the wig."

"So just take it off," my father suggested from the doorway. Although he didn't like to get involved in what he called "Dotworld," he sometimes felt obliged to show an interest.

"But I can't go out in public with my head half-shaved like this, Sam." She lifted off the wig like a hat. "I'd look like a little old man. A terminally ill man."

"You kind of would," my mother agreed.

Dot sat in the kitchen chair with the wig in her lap. She watched me chewing. "Your Uncle Mel loves those 'cots," she said.

I sensed what was coming. My mission: to convince my uncle that his place was back at home. Dot frowned down at her wig. Its silver-highlighted dark blonde curls were a frizzy, matted mess. She fingered a few strands as if trying to untangle them from the others. And that too was surely a lost cause.

"Maybe it's too tight," my father offered. "Maybe it's squeezing your brain." And with that he exited the kitchen, which he'd never really entered in the first place.

"It's not tight at all," Dot called after him. She looked at my mother and me. "It slips all over my head."

Struck by afternoon sunlight through the window, the bare top right side of Dot's skull shone. A new scar ran from her right temple straight back and then zigzagged up to the crown of her head. The horrible black stitches were gone, thank god, but the pink needle punctures were still visible. On the other side of her head, her thin gray hair was cropped short.

She had walked into a sliding glass door. I'd heard her say several times that she'd been as stupid as a stupid bird. She couldn't tell where the real world ended and the world behind glass began. She'd been flying too fast.

From the beginning, that had been the way she'd explained her accident—to Uncle Mel phoning in from Montana, and even earlier to the ER doctor who kept dutifully chuckling after each fancy tie-off of the stitches he put in her head.

"You could do embroidery, I bet," my mother had said to him. She took hold of one of Dot's hands, and I took the other. My mother and I knew that Mel and Dot were weighed down by the loss of their daughter, whom no one had seen or heard from since just before Christmas, when Jessie had borrowed a cell phone and called them. They'd missed the call but kept replaying her message. No one could understand the name of the city she said she was in. She'd saved for years—literally dimes and quarters in tips—from her barista job to travel, a forty-year-old backpacker. She was staying in hostels. She'd said she might try to find work "overseas." But in the privacy of my own thoughts over these last few months, it had begun to seem increasingly likely that Jessie was snipping the last thin thread that had held her to us. She was letting us go. I missed her too.

I squeezed Dot's hand. I didn't like watching the needle enter her scalp, but I liked seeing the doctor's elegant fingers tie the threads gently and give each one a swift little tug.

Aunt Dot had called 9-1-1 herself. Then she'd called my mother, her sister-in-law, saying she might need a ride home from the hospital.

But since I was there when the call came, I did the driving. My mother sat staring straight ahead, her ankles crossed, the toes of her loafers bobbing up and down in a steady rhythm. At stoplights I could feel her nervous bouncing make the whole car shake.

While my condo was being repainted, I'd been staying with my parents, up in my old room, where I blinked awake in the wee hours and saw the faces of my former idols—Boy George and Fat Nothing—floating around me, bobbing in the ambiguous dark waters between genders and eras, shadowy dreams and dawn's light.

And ever since her scalp-stitching, Aunt Dot had been staying in my parents' house too, in Robert's old room. With Uncle Mel "dawdling around with the dinosaurs" (Dot's words) in Montana, she was afraid to stay alone in their house—afraid, she told me, of facing more "apparitions" alone. One night, as I turned off the downstairs lights, I saw her in my dad's recliner. The last TV show had gone off, but she sat there, eyes open, seemingly stupefied by the TV's snow and hiss. She had the wig on, but it was pushed so far back on her head that it looked, from my side-angle view, like another head growing out the back of her real head. *The host head*: that was the phrase that crossed my mind.

Then, chin on her hands and still staring into the TV's sizzling static, Dot bent forward.

Someone on TV had apparently been tricked into going off into the dense woods—following a child who was running after a dog. The dog and the child were, Aunt Dot would tell us the next morning, just a "ruse." The person who'd been following them was, she reported, someone she knew, someone whom she was supposed "to catch up with and warn about a horrible deception."

"Who?" my mother asked. "Who was it?"

"Man or woman?" I asked.

Dot winced. "It was clearer last night." She touched her hands to her head, which was covered that morning with a paisley scarf. "It was all right there on TV. And I didn't even have the wig totally on." She let out a breath. "If only Mel were here." She looked up at me, her eyes as plaintive as a child's. "Maybe he'd listen to you, Lynnie."

"I don't think so. Why should he?"

"You're like a second daughter to us." A single tear was erupting in her left eye. I leaned down and patted her knuckles. This was as far as Dot had let herself touch upon the subject of my cousin Jessie.

The night before, from the dark hallway, I'd watched Dot put her head back on the recliner, and then, with two fingers, pluck the wig completely off and set it like a dead insect on the coffee table.

"Was there snow in those woods, do you remember?" I'd asked her the next morning, not really sure why I was pursuing anything so off-the-charts nuts.

Her head snapped up. "There was, Lynnie. There was snow. Just farther into the woods. In there where I lost sight of that person."

"Maybe it's time she saw a doctor," my father called from the living room. He'd turned down the TV news in order to offer his contribution for the day. "Butting heads with that window may have shook something loose."

"Like a few screws I guess he means." Dot's face was drawn, her eyes narrowed. Clearly everyone's mockery was wearing her down.

"I think we should take you back to the hospital," my mother said, as if referring to an unplayable DVD we needed to return to Blockbuster.

A Later History of Prehistory

"What I mainly want to know is what's supposed to collide with what?"

"Subatomic particles," I told Uncle Mel, "but don't ask me how."

Uncle Mel was walking fast, and I was riding slowly on a rusty blue bike he said had been his as a boy. I'd found it in the barn, and already its tires were losing the air I'd pumped—with an old hand pump—into them.

After Mel had seen a black SUV drive off the road and bump across the low brush and gopher holes, he'd grabbed something off the kitchen counter, slammed the back door, and set out walking up the dirt road that bisected what had once been a carefully kept cornfield. But that was eight centuries ago. As kids, my uncles Mel and Carl and my father had found arrowheads out there, probably from the Assiniboines. Purportedly a small group had their summer quarters here alongside what, in my Great-Grandfather Franklin Lundstrum's day, had been called Fast River, but was now called Fast Creek. A few miles south of here, it fed into the Milk River, which ran through the sleepy town of Malta.

Ahead of me Mel stopped walking, and I pedaled up beside him and stopped. We watched two men in pastel-colored short-sleeved shirts get out of the SUV and walk toward the creek bed, their heads bent over clipboards, their mouths moving.

"A newspaper I read said no one's ever seen any actual colliding going on," Mel said.

"I guess they've seen the results of collisions, though, and apparently that's all they're after."

"And it takes fifty-nine square miles underground to do that?" He nodded toward the field.

A brown truck with orange front fenders was coming toward us on the dirt road. It slowed, and then, as it pulled alongside us, the driver leaned out his window. "This supercollider thing is a joke, Mel. That rock under there has all sorts of fissures and holes. Just wait 'til they dig up a core sample and see what they're dealing with." The truck stopped, and the driver nodded to me. "Is that you? Jessie?"

Mel turned and glanced at me as if momentarily unsure himself. "This is my niece, Lynette. She's supposed to be talking some sense into me, but she's doing a terrible job."

"That about sums it up," I said, shielding my eyes but still unable to make out the driver's face in the sun's glare.

"He's Stephan Junior," Uncle Mel said finally, "old Steph's boy."

"Steve, please," he said. "Mind if I just let myself into the house, Mel? I'm going to pack up the rest of Dad's books. Then

I'll probably drive on back to Bozeman. My boy's got a soccer game in the morning."

Mel nodded. "So you're decided, then? You're selling to those collider people?"

"If they're buying, I'm selling." Steve put his truck into gear, and it lurched noisily forward. "Good luck to you, miss." He touched the bill of his baseball cap.

My father and Uncle Carl had agreed they were happy to leave it up to Mel whether, when, or to whom the Old Ranch, all 378 acres of it, should be sold. For twenty years, Mel had been the one to travel back here twice each summer—once to help Grandpa Ralph put in the hay, and then again to mow it down.

All this way up Fast Creek Road, Uncle Mel had been carrying whatever he'd grabbed from the kitchen—bundled up in a dirty blue dishtowel—in the crook of his elbow. My guess was that he'd unearthed another bone fragment from the carcass of that long-buried something I'd started calling Rex—at least, as I told Aunt Dot and my mother on the phone, for the time being. The bone fossils of two other Tyrannosaurs had been found on nearby ranches.

The men from the SUV were jotting notes on their clipboards. The one in the lavender shirt saw us and lifted his hand.

"Don't speak to them, Lynnie," Mel said. "We don't want to start anything."

"I wouldn't dream of it." I watched Mel open an edge of his towel and reach inside. When his hand emerged, it held a sandwich: dark yellow cheese on white bread. He carefully pulled the sandwich in two and handed me half.

"Here," he said. "Eat this. No arguments."

I was glad old Steph's son was clearing those boxes from Mel's dining room. I'd only been in Malta for two days, but I was already tired of maneuvering around them. Those boxes. Since his own ranch house had gone up in a wildfire fifteen years ago, the elder Mr. Severson had been renting the Lundstrum ranch. He'd just recently moved, though—into a retirement home in Bozeman.

"None of those guys knows anymore what belongs to who," Aunt Dot had told me yesterday on the phone when I mentioned the shoebox full of Army medals I'd found in the basement. "I doubt anybody could even tell you which soldier those went with, or what war."

Before I'd left Spokane, Dot had packed a cooler for me to take to Mel. Inside were a few of his favorites: blue cheese, apricots, cherries, a huge sweet Walla Walla onion, a lemon torte, a hamburger casserole. But so far he hadn't touched a thing.

As we'd put the cooler in my trunk, Dot had told me that she knew what I was getting myself into was "a royal nightmare," and for this I'd have, she added, her undying gratitude. The National Physics Foundation had made a good offer on both the adjacent Severson property and the Old Ranch. I was supposed to get Mel to "at least entertain the idea of selling." Now I was hoping that since the Seversons were selling, Steve Junior might offer a few persuasive arguments to which Uncle Mel might listen.

There were way too many "mights" in this theory, I was thinking as Mel and I stood chewing our sandwiches. Fast Creek trickled past us through a few brown cattails. I considered telling Mel—but finally didn't mention—what my mother had reported yesterday on the phone about Aunt Dot: that the doctor to whom she'd returned had mentioned bad neural connections. Dream material, he'd said, was leaking into her conscious mind. He thought other forces might "be at play" too and suggested she see a counselor and discuss her "disconnectedness." Might Dot have suffered a recent loss? the doctor had wondered aloud. Was she under increased stress?

Mel and I watched the two men trudge back to their van and get in. The van's tires made loud crunching sounds as the men drove over the dried grasses toward the road.

Suddenly a pair of huge wings flapped open. A great blue heron. Its primeval-looking talons clicked against the van's front windshield.

The van's brakes squealed. The men's heads fell forward and back. And from the shapes of their mouths, I could make out the words they shouted to each other. *What?* the one man said.

What? the other answered. *What?*

An Old-Style Sunday Dinner

The twelfth of August, my birthday, and standing in the middle of Great-Grandfather Franklin Lundstrum's former wheat field, I felt my forty-eighth year boring into me in a big hurry under the ever so slowly shrinking sun. The past kept returning, but distorted, misshapen. It had been twenty years since my husband's death, and lately when I thought of Jack, I saw a train shoot out across the horizon, a bolt of black lightning. I'd never seen the accident site. Everything that had happened once, in real time and real space, recurred now as sound around an image: the swift loud trajectory of that train, Jack's crumpling black truck. Black metal the black train kept dragging down the tracks. Quite a ways, I'd been told. The railroad company had preferred to give me money rather than information. Cash instead of facts. How many pieces he'd been broken into they wouldn't, or couldn't, say. But $217,846 was the amount of the check that came to me.

In the field of dried weeds, I tried to think myself back further, much further—into the seventy-eight-million-year-old past that Uncle Mel believed was being revealed to us, bone by bone. The pit in the ground, where I knew Mel was at that moment dusting off fossils and setting them inside a child's rusty wagon—that pit was probably thick once with water lilies and fragrant lotus. And from across Fast Creek rose an enormous something that Mel's email pal Cyber Franz proposed we might as well classify for now as a Triceratops.

I both did and didn't want to break this news to Aunt Dot. For today I planned to keep it, like an unexpected and exciting birthday gift, to myself. I tried to envision the creature's seven-foot snout dipping into the creek, which eons ago, geologists say, was the western shore of the inland Cretaceous sea.

"Hey, girl," someone shouted, and my vision blurred. The glittery subtropics became a field of weeds again.

Mel walked toward me, pulling the bone wagon behind him.

There was something else I hadn't yet told him—that I'd FedExed a fossil sample to Bozeman, to the head paleontologist at the Museum of the Rockies, and I'd sent along my cell number and asked him to call me. I'd taken matters into my own hands. I wanted facts. I wanted the fossils identified exactly.

"What I can't figure," Mel said when he caught up to me, "is how these bones didn't just wash away in the creek."

Glancing down, I saw that Mel had put a tattered patchwork quilt, which I recognized as one of his mother's, my Great-Aunt Bette's, in the bottom of the wagon. On the quilt were his tools—tiny picks and awls and brushes that looked like (and maybe had once been) dental instruments. "I'm guessing there didn't use to be a creek here," I said to Mel. "Way out there was ocean, actually"—and I pointed as if it had disappeared just yesterday. "People have found seashells, fossils of sea scorpions and sea lilies."

Mel bent over the wagon, chose a bone shard, and passed it up to me. I felt a sharp splintered edge where the piece had been recently broken.

"That's no fish, though. Right?"

"Right." I was always surprised by the bones' weightiness. It was thoroughly stone. I passed it back. A gray cloud hovered up north, maybe as far as Canada. And from that direction, I was sure I could smell rain. Slowly, then, I began explaining what I'd done with that bone sample.

Mel stood shielding his eyes with his hand so he could watch my face in the steely light.

"I only wanted to confirm what Franz told us. That's all. I wanted us to have an honest-to-god expert opinion."

Us. The word pinged like a shrill note off a tuning fork. Us. As if I were a part of the dig now, some sort of indentured assistant.

"Just so that bone comes back here the same as when it left. Just so we're clear on that." He handed me another piece. "All this"—he waved his hand above the wagon—"is our responsibility. We can't be letting parts of it go every which way."

I nodded. For a moment I thought I heard rain drumming down. I'd read that up in Drumheller, Alberta—just a hundred miles north—the skeletal remains of eighty different dinosaur species had been unearthed in a ten-acre site. Scientists thought that one of the many floods that used to ravage these plains had washed up the corpses of those drowned creatures into one bizarre mishmash.

Mel yanked on the wagon handle and started walking us south.

Us. We headed toward the squat white house in which he and Uncle Carl and my father had lived out their boyhoods. I was tired and hot and another year older. Behind us the bone wagon clattered on its tiny wheels.

As we neared the house, I saw the brown and orange pickup in the driveway.

"I guess Steve's here," Mel said.

Steve stood up from the porch step and walked to the back of his truck.

"Look what I hit," Steve called. "Now what am I supposed to do with this?" He tipped his head to me, which was a thing I'd noticed that men in this part of the West did. Then he held up a carcass by its black claw feet. A wild turkey. Its black and gray feathers shimmered.

Mel dropped the wagon handle, and we both went around to the back of the truck.

"I almost hit some of those myself a couple days ago," I said. "They're everywhere."

"If you pluck her, you can eat her," Mel told Steve. "But if she's an old one, she might be a tad tough."

"*She,*" I said and leaned closer to the turkey.

Steve dropped it back in the truck. "I swerved to miss about five of these suckers, but I guess this one—"

"It is so a she," Mel said. "See those wattles. That ain't a tom."

Steve turned and smiled at me. "I think your brother and I—is his name Robbie?—used to shoot cap guns." The tan skin around his eyes crinkled.

"Robert," I said. "Yeah, we came here in the summers when we were kids."

"I'll bet Lynnie knows how to pluck that bird." Mel turned the turkey over in the truck. "There's not a damn thing wrong with it."

"Her," I said.

Watching those wild turkeys on the road into town last week, I'd suddenly understood how the odd evolutionary step from dinosaur to bird made sense. With their rounded bodies, tiny heads, and gangly legs, those turkeys did resemble the dinosaurs in Mel's books. As my car headed directly at them, they'd just taken their time waddling off the road—too tired, it seemed, to even try to fly.

"I could help," Steve said. "Do we just yank off the feathers? Is that the idea?"

Mel winked at me.

I couldn't help laughing. "We'll scald it first," I told Steve. "That'll make life easier."

Mel shook his head. "Well, if she's going to be ate, she shouldn't be sitting here in the sun."

"Do you have a big enough kettle?" I called after him.

He waved a hand behind him. "It's right where it's been for fifty years." At the porch stoop, he turned. "Girl, can you first get those bones stowed in the barn?"

"Okay," I called. "Follow me," I said to Steve, noticing he wore sandals, not the cowboy boots I'd been expecting. "We may as well put the turkey in the shade 'til Mel gets the water ready."

"Bones?" Steve said. "Did he mean the turkey?"

"No, he means these actual bones." I walked around to the wagon and picked up the handle.

Steve, dangling the turkey by its claws, bent toward the wagon. "What died?"

"Now, that—*that's* the million-dollar question."

"Holy shit," Steve said when we'd stepped inside the barn. He set the turkey down and stared at the bones Mel had laid carefully on two-by-four planks atop sawhorses—a makeshift display that stretched the sixty-foot length of the barn. "He's done a lot of work on that critter since I saw it last. That's gotta be a mastodon. Right?"

"That's *one* of the prevailing theories."

Steve laughed and moved closer to a group of bones Mel believed was a rump. "You gotta give it to Mel. He's no quitter."

"He thinks if he can get this sucker completely reconstructed, he might be able to find it a home in a museum. Then and only then might he be able to let the whole ranch go. And I stress the word *might*."

Steve turned to me. "Only two thousand years ago, tribal people out here were still hunting mastodons with spears. Two thousand years—that's nothing." He ran his fingers along a glued seam between two bones that I doubted had ever really been one and the same.

From our opposite ends of the long display, we stared across the pieced-together stone bones with their many empty slots and holes. "Whatever it was," I said, "it probably came here to forage for food, or, who knows, maybe just to die."

"There's a lot missing," Steve said. "A lot." His voice echoed in the cool barn. "Judging from these hind legs, this thing must have been over twelve feet tall. On second thought, that might actually be too tall for a mastodon."

⑥

Cooking, I felt energized, even in the heat. I'd shoved sprigs of rosemary and thyme (brought from home) under the turkey's skin. Steve wandered in and out of the kitchen, offering to be a taster, an onion chopper, an uncorker of the bottle of wine I'd brought. In the kitchen there was work to do that I actually understood. Basting the turkey, I'd turned, humming, and found Steve watching me from the doorway. He'd been packing the last of his father's books—those dusty Louis L'Amour novels, *Showdown at Yellow Butte*, *Lonely on the Mountain*, *Flint*, and *The Trail to Seven Pines*—and he had a black marking pen in his hand.

"What was that song?" he asked.

Suddenly I couldn't remember its name or any of the notes that came next.

Steve, waiting, popped the cap on and off the pen. His eyes were a shock of blue.

I shrugged. "Probably one of my dad's little fishing ditties." I heard myself chirp a nervous little laugh, keenly aware but not sure why I didn't want him to leave the doorway. I didn't want him to stop watching me.

"Sam Lundstrum—I'll bet he's up in Alaska right now," Steve offered.

I sprinkled the bird with chives and tarragon, happy discoveries I'd found growing wild behind the barn. "No, my mother pestered him to retire, and he finally has."

Steve smiled. "My dad—he may have known that, but he's having trouble remembering things. Last month he put his foot on the gas instead of the brake at the bottom of your hill. In case you were wondering what happened to the mailbox."

"Mel mentioned that."

"That's when I moved him to the Good Samaritan. He's giving those sisters a true test of their Christian charity." He nodded then to the turkey I was about to put back in the oven. "That's a nice-looking bird. Obviously you know what you're doing."

Later, sitting outside since the kitchen was so hot, the three of us polished off nearly half the turkey, which Mel declared hadn't been so old after all. I brought out the last of the apricots and passed them around in a china bowl.

"Dee-licious," Steve said. "I've never tasted apricots like these." He turned the seed over between his fingers.

I tried not to watch him so intently. His soft voice and easygoing manner had grown on me awfully fast. Too fast, I thought. Quit staring.

"They're from Washington," Mel told him. "Greenbluff. That's orchard country. Lynette brought them."

"They're actually from Aunt Dot," I said.

"Yeah? How's she doing?" Steve asked.

"Dot had a run-in with a door," Mel said, "and now she sees little green men. Isn't that right, Lynnie?"

"Not entirely."

Steve helped himself to another apricot and shot me a raised-eyebrow look.

"She says she's headed home soon," I said to Mel, "*your* home."

"Glad to hear it." Mel put the apricot he'd been about to eat back in the bowl. I tried to keep my gaze on that lovely bowl.

Over a hundred years ago, someone had painted the most delicate lavender flowers on it.

"Things would be better for Dot with you there," I said. "Back in Spokane."

Steve nodded, chewing slowly. There was something about his presence here—this impartial third party, I thought—that made it easier, finally, for Mel and me to navigate around the rocky questions.

"I've got plenty that needs doing right here," Mel said.

"I wouldn't mind coming back one day and giving you a hand with those bones," Steve suddenly offered.

Mel glanced at him and then at me. "Maybe by October those reactor people can take over here. I'm sure they'll make a holy mess of things."

Steve helped himself to another apricot. "Are these U-pick?"

"They certainly weren't me-pick," I said.

"Where's your boy?" Mel turned to Steve. "Wasn't he going to help you today?"

"He's with his mother this weekend."

And then it hit me: Ah, yes, there was, of course, a wife. Mother of Steve's son. For no reason that made sense, all the evening's events—the defeathering of the turkey, the cooking, the eating, the show-and-tell in the barn about the bones—all that had chased off the fact that there must be a wife. She was back there in Bozeman. Then something quite different occurred to me: he hadn't called her *wife*.

Mel leaned toward the apricots, sorted among the few that were left, and picked one. He bit into it.

Steve and I watched his response, but Mel only stared straight ahead as he chewed. I was thinking we'd crossed a major hurdle here. I had an estimated date of departure (EDD) from Mel—October—that I could tell Dot.

Steve tipped his chair back. "So if I can't get you to sing me one of your little songs, maybe you'll tell me some more about Robert . . . what he's done with his life."

We sat outside, letting the evening chill cool us. Mel and I filled Steve in on Robert, now a landscape architect in Seattle. He and his partner, Jake, had their own firm.

"Life partner," Mel chipped in, and Steve and I smiled at each other. Mel could surprise you.

It had taken my brother a long time to quit trying to be what he thought others expected, but as he'd gradually allowed himself—the *undeniable one,* as I used to think of it to myself—to emerge, he'd also gradually reconnected to all us Lundstrums. *Love is love,* I remember Aunt Dot saying to my parents and Uncle Mel one Christmas Eve as Robert and Jake wrapped presents in the other room. That was twenty years ago, but it seemed like last night.

Then I offered Steve the short version of my post-screwy-Lasik-surgery life: groping my way like a blind woman down the streets of Spokane. Steve told us how he and his wife, Patty, had had "a recent parting of the ways," and he grew animated and was clearly a proud dad when he talked about his boy Luke, apparently "something of a phenom on the clarinet."

"That turkey," Steve said as we took our dishes back inside, "had been a grand dame, but she's gone to a good cause."

Boxes of old tax returns, of chipped china plates, tarnished knives, and bent forks. Steve kept packing whatever he recognized as his father's. He'd appeared Saturday at the back door, early. On some of the boxes he'd put a big black *G*—for Goodwill, he said. Later that morning, the ones marked with a black *X* were going to the Malta dump.

I made hotcakes, which is what Montanans call pancakes. In the kitchen I felt reconnected to my old life, although I'd begun to miss it less. Marlene was taking care of everything at the Chef's Pal just fine. She called me every other evening to report in. She liked being in charge, and she was good at it. Over hotcakes, Mel and Steve were cordial. We ate off the old dishes I'd found in the cellar. Years of dust had fallen off them when I'd dipped them in the hot suds.

"Good idea," Mel had said when he'd come in from digging yesterday and seen them drying on the counter. "It's about time those old dishes of my mother's got some use."

"I'll be careful with them," I said.

"Do I look worried? What were they ever being saved for, anyway?"

Over hotcakes, I'd asked Steve if there was a specialty food store in Bozeman. I wanted more fresh herbs, better lettuce, and I was hoping to find some almond butter, none of which the small Safeway in Malta carried.

"There's a health food store," Steve said, "but I can't say for sure if they'll have what you're after."

"Well, I'm going to try it," I said. "Besides, I've never really seen Bozeman."

"If you came on Wednesday, there's an afternoon concert at the high school," Steve said. "It's a visiting string quartet from Fargo. They've invited Luke to play a small solo part. He's been nervous about it for a month."

"How great for him, though." I turned to Mel. "Do you need anything in Bozeman?"

He shook his head, keeping my face in his gaze. Later, after Steve had driven off with the boxes I'd helped him rope into his truck bed, Mel came in from the barn and stood in the middle of the kitchen watching me. I was drying a soup tureen. I was planning on making turkey soup with the leftovers.

"I've got nothing against Steve, but just think about what you're doing, Lynnie. Just give it some hard thought." Mel had in his hand a huge femur he'd pieced together from splinters. I knew it was one that Grandpa Ralph had begun reconstructing fifty years ago. Now it was finally complete.

"Don't blow it out of proportion." I opened a cupboard door. "Steve's just proud of his kid. He wants me to hear him play." But I was actually a little nervous. Was this a date? Had Steve himself stopped to think that it might be awkward to introduce me to his son? And why *should* it be? Maybe, halfway back to Bozeman by now, he was sorry he'd offered to meet me at the high school. I put the tureen in the cupboard and turned around.

Mel had set the femur on the kitchen table. He'd recently received a special quick-drying glue called Vinac from the Fossils R Us website. I recognized the smell. I bent over the bone, recalling what Aunt Dot had said the morning I'd left Spokane: "I doubt that whatever he's digging up in that god-forsaken place is much more prehistoric than he is."

"Poor guy," I said to Steve about Luke. My heart went out to the boy. "I'll just stay here." I touched Steve's arm. The concert was over, and we'd gone backstage to see Luke, but realizing how upset he was, I'd held back at the edge of the red velvet curtains. The boy's lips shook. He was on the verge of tears. Onstage he'd gotten ahead of himself in the solo part and had to stop and start again. Now the mustached cellist from the quartet was trying to tell him that no one had noticed, but clearly the boy knew this wasn't true. Adults just made themselves look ridiculous lying like that to kids.

I stepped farther into the curtain folds that felt like thick, cool rain and watched as Steve took his son in his arms. The mustached man seemed glad to walk away, to join the two women and the other man from the quartet who were putting their instruments into cases.

Steve was saying something into the boy's ear. Then Luke stepped out of his father's embrace and held up the clarinet. He touched a valve. Then Steve did too, gently, as if it were a piece of silver from Tut's tomb. I could see that Luke had Steve's blue eyes, brightened now, I supposed, by the welled-up tears.

I thought possibly the tears hadn't been solely about the mishap with the music, but maybe had to do with the darker mishap of the boy's parents' life together recently ripped in two like a sheet of tissue paper. I recalled how tough Uncle Carl and Aunt Mary's divorce had been on poor Buster, the way he would suddenly shout at Jessie or Robert or me over seemingly nothing and then stalk off in a huff. We had to love him all the harder, my mother would tell us. Now Buster and Mitka were about to have their third child. They'd settled in Anaheim and seemed happy—even, as Uncle Carl told everyone, "prosperous." And Buster was "done, thank God, being the Beast," Middy had told me on the phone, and was now "skating as all kinds of mouses Mr. Walt Disney ever dreamed up."

Steve laid his tan hand on Luke's shoulder, and then all at once she was there, the woman I assumed was the wife, Patty. She had a long braid of dark brown hair down her back. She kissed Luke's cheek.

The quartet members nodded to me as they made a quiet exit past me. "Wonderful," I said to them, trying to recall the Bach, the crescendoing music, and the rickety auditorium seats, and how I'd felt like a high school girl myself amid such a crowd, especially with Steve's presence next to me like a pulse of heat. I'd slid my sandaled feet—covered in white flour—under the seat in front of me. While we'd waited for the music to begin, he'd drawn me a map to the Bozeman Food Co-op. He'd drawn in the stoplights as asterisks, noting the number of them I'd encounter. His tan hands brushing mine as he handed me the map sent a jolt of adrenaline through me.

Now I felt in my pocket for the map and began to back away from the curtain. I backed away from the backstage where two parents leaned together and comforted their boy. I walked down a small set of stairs, pushed open a door, and stepped into the parking lot. The musicians were laughing now, loading their instruments into a van. I was sure Steve would be grateful not to have to introduce me to his family. Clearly he had his hands full. I found my car and backed out of the lot, driving into the hot day and the surprisingly heavy Bozeman traffic.

The Food Co-op proved to be a better one, I thought, than any in Spokane. I gathered ingredients, things to add to that soup when I returned to Malta: fresh organic zucchinis, red peppers, and large, lovely shallots. Later, driving north on Route 59, I realized how tired I was. The muddled Bach, Luke's tears, Steve's long tanned fingers, and even my cousin Jessie's face—all began to blur in my mind. I hit 90 mph across the Central Plains, skirting the Little Rockies and the Charles M. Russell National Wildlife Refuge. Jessie. I was worried that by now my uncle had put the pieces of her life together . . . as I had. And if he had, I suspected that, like me, he couldn't bring himself to say what he saw now. And what he knew, what he'd come to know, was something Dot hadn't, and maybe never would. And this rift in knowledge was widening the sea between them.

There'd been so much about my cousin's life—last year in that Spokane apartment with the horrid lime-green carpet—that I had simply not permitted myself to think might be true. There'd been two women Jessie shared that place with—each with her own bedroom, while Jessie slept in the living room behind a fabric screen. The last time I visited her there, she was preparing a chicken to go in the oven, although if we were going to eat it before I had to leave for work, it should have already been cooking. "Sorry," Jessie said when I pointed that out, "I guess I overslept." The apartment was rank with smoke. Cigars, I guessed. Candy and Ruthann had been in their bedrooms with the doors closed, although it was almost noon. There were stains on the green carpet that hadn't been there when I'd visited once before. Condom wrappers on a window ledge.

"How can you let them do that here?" I'd asked her. "There're children in this building."

"*Let* them," Jessie said. "Yeah, right." She was sprinkling the chicken with paprika. The carcass had gone completely red.

"One of these days there'll be cops up here. Then you'll all be in trouble—not just those two." I nodded toward the rooms down the hall.

"It doesn't happen that often. Things were a little tight this month. Candy got her hours cut at the bakery, and Ruthann had to buy her kid some school clothes."

"Her kid?"

"Yeah, he's out east somewhere with the grandmother. Benito is his name." She shoved the chicken into the oven and lit a cigarette.

"*Benito.* Like Mussolini? God, what a name."

Jessie shrugged. "She calls him the Bean."

Jessie had wanted her bangs and the back of her long hair trimmed, and she'd asked me to stop by with my scissors. This was something we'd done for each other for half our lives. But I could see that she was sorry now that she'd asked. She stared through the oven's greasy black door.

That day kept replaying in my mind: Jessie's hair still damp, the sweet smell of the roasting chicken. She wore a pair of silver earrings that had tiny softly jingling bells. If only the girls in the bedrooms hadn't awakened. If only they hadn't shouted those silly comments to Jessie about someone they called the *little fart* and how it was a good thing the Rev had found someone just Jessie's size. *The Rev knows. The Rev rocks.* The girls had no idea I was standing there in the kitchen. *Jessie's itsy-bitsy boy*, they'd taunted. Jessie yelled at them to *Shut the hell up.* Then one of them was suddenly standing in the hallway—laughing, naked, a thin gray rubber tube cinched around her arm. She saw me and frowned. Her short red hair was combed straight up from her head.

No doubt I'd erased that part of the scene—at least for a while—from my mind. Instead I'd remembered that the girls had showered quietly, and Jessie had stopped smoking long enough for me to trim her bangs. We'd talked about Cousin Fran's cataracts, and I'd tried to explain what those were and what the doctor's procedure would be. I'd learned more about eyes than I wanted to.

Months passed. I hadn't seen Jessie again. No one had. No one we knew.

"Doesn't a cataract mean a rock too?" Jessie had asked me that day when I'd gotten around to the back of her long hair.

"I already said *yes* to that," I snapped. The scissors made a sound like notes a bird might try to sing before it's learned the real tune.

The Nature of the Species

The phone rang early in the morning and late at night. Uncle Mel wasn't speaking to Dot. If she called and he answered, he'd hand the phone to me without saying a word. Often Dot didn't even ask about him but reported instead to me about something she'd "seen." Recently, for instance, there'd been a ship with white sails and a girl trying to cram a glass bottle twice its size into its hull. The bottle was somehow to fit within the ship. "But how was a mystery," Dot said. "So was why."

"I can't imagine what it means."

"Nobody can, honey." She let out a long sigh. "I just don't want to live like this the rest of my life. That's what bothers me most."

"Are you seeing the counselor?"

"He thinks Jessie might even be dead, and says I have to consider that. He gave me a book. It's called a 'grief workbook.' It reminds me of third grade. I have to fill in blanks. Lots of blanks. I just wish to god I didn't have to do it all on my own."

Talking to Dot made me miss Jessie even more. I could recall the exact way she used to say my name—Lyn-KNEE!—that tone of surprise and mockery and delight. Since she'd gone missing, twice in dreams I'd heard her shout my name in that I-want-an-answer-fast voice, and both times I'd startled awake with the same thought: if only I'd stayed asleep, I might have heard what she'd been about to ask me.

"I don't think she's dead," Dot said. "I think I'd know if she was dead."

I heard her inhale from her cigarette. She was in their home again, alone up there in the lake cabin with the acrylic eyes of a dozen mounted heads watching her. I'd grown up among those somethings, and, like acquaintances, some I liked and some I didn't. The quirky little green-throated mallard and the up-for-any-shenanigans red fox were a couple of old friends. But the razorback boar and the vulture I still gave, as all through my girlhood, a wide berth.

"Finishing this thing with the dinosaur bones seems to be really important to Mel," I told her. "He has this idea he's the caretaker of all that's out there."

"Bullcrap."

"I'm not sure," I heard myself snap back. "It's coming together; it's got these short little front legs and much, *much* longer back ones, and—"

"Well it sounds like you two are in hog heaven," she said. "Look, Lynnie, I gotta go. I have three more pages in my workbook to finish. Tell Mel the fish out here are biting."

After we hung up, I checked Mel's computer (which was my old one) and saw there was another email from Cyber Franz. He sent a couple every day—long-winded advice on tools, descriptions of and links to other fossil websites and nearby digs in progress. I was amazed at how quickly Mel had picked up the computer's many uses for research and communication with strangers. Today's first missive from Franz was about a site from which Mel could purchase the apparently very necessary air scribe, a miniature jackhammer. After Franz had himself a peek at the newest digital photos that I'd helped Mel download and send, he fired back that the creature was looking increasingly like a *Struthiomimus altus*. Alive sixty million years ago, it had resembled an enormous ostrich. Its tail acted as a counterweight to the bird-o-saur's top-heavy front. Cyber Franz always ended his emails with quotes from a Bible verse—something from Revelations or Leviticus. Everything Franz himself was unearthing on his own ranch down in Utah he thought were the dregs of the last unholy days of earth. Earth before God's previous reckoning. Before the flood. Cyber Franz was driving me nuts.

"All that holy reckoning baloney makes me less inclined to believe what he's saying about the Struthiomimus," I told Mel. I'd gone out to the barn, where he was brushing Paleo-Bond adhesive on the chevron-shaped bones of the tail. We guessed that the tail, all fossilized now by silica, probably weighed half a ton. The wind hissed through cracks between the wide barn planks.

"I just look around all that God talk, Lynnie," Mel said. "You can too."

"There's getting to be a heck of a lot of it to look around."

Mel didn't answer. With an X-Acto knife he was cleaning sand off a shard. He had a steady hand, a keen focus. This was why he'd made a good living as a taxidermist. Standing near the other end of the creature, I glanced down into its skull cavity. A hard black stone. Also incomplete. Maybe three-fifths of a head. There was, yes, as Steve had pointed out, so much unfinished—not just in the past, but right here in the present. The skull made me wince.

"There we go," Mel said. "Beautiful!" The shard he'd just placed into a tail vertebra fit perfectly.

I nodded. Behind him on another table were piles of fossil bones he didn't know what to do with, bones that clearly didn't belong to this thing slowly taking shape.

He handed me the glue, and taking up a Q-tip, I glued. All afternoon, I glued.

Down by Fast Creek, where Mel's excavation—a continuation of Grandpa Ralph's—was still going on, were, as we'd come to understand, some altogether *other* fossilized somethings, probably the younger *Struthiomimus altuses*. The mother had died curled up atop her dying brood.

As the half-moon rose, I stood outside talking to Dot again, this time on my cell.

Poor Dot, I thought. There she was by herself in Spokane, Spokane of the underworld, Spokane with the pictures of a daughter in her prom dress. Jessie's long auburn hair has been done up high on her head with trailing wisps of curls, Jessie in a canoe, as a Brownie, Jessie skating with her cousin Buster, or with me, wearing our matching aprons. Pictures scattered on the walls among the elk heads and deer antlers. The snarling cougar.

This was the place to which Aunt Dot wanted Mel to return: to stand among the many expressions of ire, regret, sorrow, farewell—all stuck, changeless. Dot's voice rambled on in my ear. More visions. Armies of ants. I was exhausted, half-asleep on my feet.

In the Greek story, Demeter keeps looking for the one she's lost. In my own last night's dream, she called *Jess-sseee? Jesssseee.* Then *Mel, Mel.* She called mellifluously. Melodically.

But the ones she's lost can't hear. Too much nightshade. Narcissus. What flowers had the child gathered? What had the child eaten? A chasm in the earth opens; a hand reaches up. Goodbye, kiddo. So long. Someone's plunging a shovel into the earth. Another is casting the first stones. Running water over bones. Humming to bones.

Lady, keep your wig on, I'd been saying to myself after I'd told her not to worry and turned the cell phone off. *Lady, can't you see I'm way the hell out here, and a great lake of water and ice is headed this way?*

"Come here for a sec," Steve said. "You've got something in your hair." We were standing in the driveway.

When I stepped closer, he tipped my chin down. I could smell his aftershave, something citrusy and clean. His hands, though, smelled of the damp earth. We'd been helping Mel clean bones in the barn, and now it was late, and Steve was about to head back to Bozeman.

"Just a leaf, I think." He ran his fingers through the top of my hair and then carefully lifted something out.

"God, I hope it's not a spider," I said. And then, without thinking, I put my right hand on his chest, my palm open and flat against his blue T-shirt. "I hate spiders," I said, my voice shaky, my breathing too fast. "I don't mind other bugs, but—"

"Look—it's a leaf, really."

I raised my head.

He moved his hand down in front of my eyes. And there was the leaf—a tiny brown one pinched between his fingers. He smiled. His blue eyes seemed almost purple in the dimming light.

"I'd never have pegged you as someone scared of spiders." He brushed the leaf across my nose. "Maybe I should check to be sure you're completely de-leafed." He flicked the brown leaf away and put his fingers back into my hair.

Through my palm I could feel his heart ticking. I took a breath and closed my eyes as if considering a dive from a cliff into deep black water.

He kissed my forehead. "This might be a little dangerous," he whispered.

I couldn't speak. I moved my hand across his chest, my fingertips touching his neck. I could hardly breathe.

His lips against mine were soft and tentative. Then he moved away slowly as if the kiss had made him drowsy. He shook his head. But the "no" of his gesture seemed more a caution to himself than to me.

I found a handful of words. "I guess I'm complicating your life," I said. "I'm sorry."

"Well, you *have* complicated it." His face bore a trace of a smile. Why *had* I said that bit about being sorry? *Was* I? The air was cooling fast. I had no idea what else to say. I lifted my hand from his chest.

He took it. "I'm happy," he said. "That's what's so complicated."

I stared over his shoulder, blinking up into that hazy half-moon. I didn't understand him. I didn't understand any of this. My pulse was still racing.

"I'm not used to that." He held my eyes. "Happy, I mean." His lips brushed my knuckles.

After Steve drove away, I sat on the back stoop. The half-moon lit up half the sky like a far-off crime light. From the gnarled cottonwoods near the creek bank, a barn owl hooted. How odd, I thought, for someone to be surprised by his own happiness. And that's when I realized I wasn't. I was not surprised by my own. It had, in small increments, crept over me, gradually undoing me from the old grief—first over Jack, and now, slowly, over losing Jessie. These last few mornings, I'd awakened imagining conversations that Steve and I might have. I varied the lines. There was, each day, a little more sexual innuendo in the exchanges I invented between us. I could almost feel on the inside of my left thigh the place I'd imagined his hand last night and this morning his mouth.

The screen door behind me squeaked open. Mel stepped out and stood on the top step. "He's married, you know?"

"Got it," I told him. "He's still wearing the ring."

"He has a kid."

"I've got the picture, Mel."

"Do you?"

Mel's voice was crisp in the muggy air. "You're headed down a dangerous path. That's just my opinion."

The kiss had been *sort* of an accident. If Mel mentioned another thing about Steve, that's what I'd say. Since no doubt Mel had seen the kiss. He didn't miss much. Or maybe I was already explaining it to myself that way. "You're a grown woman."

"Yeah, Mel, I am."

An accident. There was something, though, that I planned never to tell: I had put the leaf in my own hair. For Steve to see. For Steve to lift out. For his hand's touch. Such was the kind of covert thing only a woman overwhelmed by her own desire was capable of doing.

The Task Ahead

The just-rising red ball of sun was staring me down at eye level. I was walking, powerwalking, straight into it. The thoughts a person tries not to think are, naturally, the ones that most press in. How weirdly fitting that I'd be drawn to a married man— since his marital status was, of course, the perfect excuse for me to steer clear of him. It'd be best, I told myself, to pack my car, to take off, and get myself cleanly away from Malta.

I'd been talking to Marlene about postponing our big end-of-summer sale at the Chef's Pal, but she wanted to proceed as usual. For me, although the barn full of bones still felt dizzying, daunting, and utterly exhausting, it called me to it each day with a new eagerness. Something very like a bird wanted to fly out of there. And like a silly teenager, I couldn't block the kiss from my mind: that ploy of the plucked leaf just before my breath stopped. My dismay. My delight.

Clearly those two old discordant feelings had trailed me here—out of adolescence and into adulthood. I recognized their unforgettably jarring notes struck at the same moment. *Just try it,* my brother had badgered me once, wanting me to eat what I'd sworn I wouldn't: the sweet, nutty meat of a dove. Robert and my father had gotten up before dawn to go hunting. The beautiful doves . . . and me almost in tears the night before, begging them to *please, please don't kill those birds.* I was nine. I knew the men would rip the breasts—just the breasts— off the doves and leave the rest of the carcasses under the trees for the crows to ravage. Robert had demonstrated the ripping motion with his hands as if it were a thing I might one day do. I'd frowned at him. But later there'd been that delicious smell from the grill out back, and I'd been so hungry. A small, mildly herbed dove breast was set on my plate and passed to me. I wasn't going to touch it, but I bent and sniffed it. My mouth watered. My father nodded and my mother smiled. However much I didn't want to eat it, suddenly it seemed impossible not to. I watched my knife slice carefully in toward the dove's pale breastbone. I savored every mouthful. I hated my hunger.

I was far away in my thoughts, loopy mini-lectures—*No, you can't keep flirting with him; quit it*—as I walked quickly up a small rise. I was probably feeling sorry for myself more than I was actually missing what I couldn't have in my life. But if a person understands all this, as I obviously did, what was the purpose of giving oneself a good talking-to? It was a bright early morning. Not yet hot, but certainly quite warm. At the top, I was in mid-stride and moving too fast to stop.

And then it was too late to stop.

There isn't any way to make this NOT happen.

That's what flashed through my mind as I pulled up short. I was way too close to it—the coil of it—golden brown, black diamonds down its back. I was too near the hiss and the raised tail. Too close to the rattle.

Even stepping back or sideways, I'd still be within striking distance.

Blunt nose, dark stripes on either side of the triangular head. When a thing so beautiful comes at you, was there something else to do but close your eyes?

Whoa was what I heard my voice say. Maybe I'd tried to duck back at the moment it struck. Maybe I'd jumped. I don't recall. I do remember that the bite felt more like a blow. Like brass knuckles punching my calf.

Had I screamed? Probably not.

I stood there frozen, afraid to look at my leg, to move it or touch it, afraid to breathe. And suddenly it was hard to breathe. That can't be good, I thought. Then I saw the pool of blood beneath the rattler's pale yellow underbelly. Oh. He'd been hit by a car and was partially stuck to the road. That explained why he hadn't taken off when he heard me coming.

The snake stuck his head under his own belly.

Now how long will I live?

That was a recurring thought between the short curses I let out in quick breaths in the middle of Fast Creek Road. Had I cursed the snake first? Or God? Had I called for help before limping like a wounded raccoon to the side of the road?

None of that's clear. I recall limping to the edge of the gravel, turning, and looking down the hill, then back up, uncertain which way I'd just come. Which was the way back to the Lundstrum ranch? At some point I crumpled to a heap—fetal, small, a dot on a road that wasn't even on a map. I was cold; the sun bearing down made me cold.

I'm going to freeze to death in this heat. That's what I woke up thinking as I came to in the Cornerstone Café, where, evidently, just as Dr. Wyatt had been about to dig into his hotcakes, a mail carrier named Jimmy Tallman had pulled me out of his pickup truck, carried me through the café, and laid me like a roast on a butcher-block table in the kitchen.

When you are a woman passed out in the greasy kitchen of a Montana café full of coffee-drinking men at 8 A.M., perhaps not surprisingly, all your needs are met. The cold, clean dishtowel to the forehead, the sneakers unlaced and gently tugged loose. The hands patted. Any wound is soothed, any pain anesthetized.

A bitten woman lies there on the table where later in the morning onions will be chopped and chicken livers glazed, and she'll recall, yes, something quite striking had indeed struck, struck hard, something malevolently handsome, and she had, yes, simply stepped toward it . . . like a task ahead.

When, for that brief moment out there on the road, I'd glanced down at my calf, I'd seen the two holes. A rattler has reserve fangs—how nice for him—so if one breaks off, well, no cause for alarm. The forked fang, the two tines of a skewer, had lifted the oblivious biped off the road and dropped her here on the Cornerstone Café's cutting table. Something that needed basting. Good thing there was that oversized oven.

Oww, oww, oww, I called into the kitchen.

I could feel the fangs' two holes. Into one flowed the kitchen noise—*She's Mel's girl. No, she's gone; this one's Sam's kid, you know, the one who lost her husband, oh her, is that a radio on her belt, get that radio off her. Isn't this one named Jeanette? Hold this blood pressure cuff, Jesus, just let me get this first. Yeah, yeah, the serum's always in my bag. Hey, we're going to drive you to the hospital in Bozeman. Somebody call Sam. Okay, then, call Mel; hell, call one of them Lundstrums. Here comes the shot now, missy. You'll be good to go in a sec.*

And from the other hole, since apparently my mouth was clamped shut, trickled my answers. *Go away and let me sleep. The leg is killing me. I'm sorry, Jessie. It was my fault you fell from Grandpa Ralph's dock; I never told you, yes, I tripped you. It wasn't funny when you banged your head and were all wet to boot. Your mother's in stitches. This leg hurts. Please take the leg away. There's a dinosaur in the barn, and no saddle seems to fit him. If I were dead, I'd give that rattler a piece of my mind. But which? The piece of me he made afraid? Let me think. Jessie, I hope you're finding this whole debacle a riot. I hope you're laughing your head off.*

I had lain in a heap on the road—for how long, I'll never know for sure. I'd be told later it couldn't have been more than ten minutes before Jimmy Tallman found me—since if it had been much longer, everyone said, I'd be dead. The sun bore down. I remember that, that and a mild queasiness and struggling to catch my breath. In my mind, though, and for that stretch of time, I believed I was dying, I was sure I was dying at the beach.

The beach had a cool breeze, and I had this idea the breeze would blow me out of the bright heat. There'd be an ocean when I stood up again—dead, I supposed—and I could wade into it. The beach wouldn't be just a memory. It wouldn't be just behind my closed eyes. On it Jessie and I would be walking again in our new two-piece swimsuits, with our middles bare and slim and tan. We'd have those pink beginnings of breasts, what I'd heard my father whisper to Robert were "sprouts," and the sprouts weren't to be looked at, he'd said, not even a fleeting glance.

Waking again, I had the word *venom* on my mind, *venomous.* Opening my eyes, I expected to find myself still in the Cornerstone Café. I expected to see staring down at me the cook, Charlie Boyd, and Dr. Wyatt—one with a steak knife and one with a scalpel. But instead I saw a nurse. She leaned over me.

"You've been whispering something about the beach," she said. "I usually dream about that too, but mostly in the winter."

"You've still got your leg is the good news." Mel stepped around the nurse.

"What hospital is this?" I asked.

"It's a medical center," the nurse said. "We don't use the word *hospital*. By the way, I believe I went on a date with your brother once. Robbie."

"Robert?" I tried to raise myself, wondering where he was. I saw his long black eyelashes flutter. Shouldn't he be here, maybe handing me a Coke? Had he gone to college now? Had I?

A voice floated across the white room. *We've got her plenty doped up.*

I'm here, Lynnie.

What?

She said she's fine. She's going to drift a little. I guess that's good to do at the beach.

Lynnie, it's Uncle Mel. You sat a long time on that road before Jimmy found you.

Mel?

It's okay. You go on back to sleep, girl. I'm watching out here.

Was it winter? "I'm cold," I said. If it was winter in hell, what was Mel doing here? What was *here*? How did the story go? There was Aunt Dot wading around in the shallow end; she had on her Pluto costume; she was carrying a huge tined spear. *Here* was Montana.

I'll go get her another blanket.

No, *here* was a field of flowers on the plain of Enna, in Sicily, and Uncle Mel was out there picking. A tisket, a tasket, a million bones in his basket. Why was Robert's friend Jake standing amid the flowers? Why was he holding Robert's hand?

Your mother's going to kill me, Lynnie.

"No, but Aunt Dot . . . Aunt Dot's looking for you." Those bones. Ezekiel's bones. Wasn't that what crazy Cyber Franz said? They'd rise again. And if it's spring in Hades, it's okay for a girl to be here, here in her childhood. And Jessie's too. Here with the boy Steve, who'd stabbed my leg with a fork. He hadn't meant to. It was an accident.

Steve? Steve's not here, Lynette. Christ.

Here's a blanket. We'll warm her up.

Warmed-up turkey tastes delicious. Bright red-streaked feathers yanked out, and Steve's hands, and leaning toward him and kissing as the eye of the moon watched. The eye was out there on the porch. It had seen. "Mel?"

"Trust me. You're fine now."

"Did you see it?"

"They'll never find that snake, honey. He's long gone to the buzzards."

Everything Happens at Once

I missed television. I was recuperating, lying in the upstairs heat of the old ranch house and wishing I could watch some talking heads tell me what to think about the world. I had never dreamed there'd be a time I would miss TV.

The first time I remember registering a television's presence in my life, it was because my mother was kneeling in front of one, sobbing. I was four years old, and I couldn't tell if she wanted to crawl into it or take it in her arms. I turned my face toward its light.

Horses. High-stepping horses.

I put my hand on my mother's shoulder, and she reached up—not looking away from the screen—and patted it. The horses pulled a wagon with a flag-draped box. A hurt emanated from that box, a hurt that was curiously *not* of the body, but stultifying nonetheless. And when I looked harder, when I really looked, that box the horses pulled yanked me to my knees too.

What just the day before had been black-and-white flickerings—barely discernible as even light waves—were now, I realized, figures. People. I saw they were families: the mothers, my mother, weeping; the children's faces bore a solemnity I suddenly understood; their eyes held my exact same dread, which was new and seemed capable of combustion.

And those pounding hooves. Horses were coming gracefully down the road, through our living room, and right past the two of us kneeling there, the matching ponytails hanging down our backs. The taller-headed one leans toward the smaller one and whispers, *There he goes, honey. That was our president. There. That was him. Now he's gone.*

When I came downstairs, the supercollider guys were sitting in armchairs across from Uncle Mel on the living room couch. I'd cleaned up that room, packed away trinkets, sent the broken recliner to Goodwill in the back of Steve's truck. I wondered if Mel had asked the men for more time, or more money. I couldn't imagine what made their faces so taut.

I went to the kitchen and limped back to the living room with a tray, a pitcher of iced tea, and some extra glasses the men helped me set on the coffee table. I was thinking I liked this room now. All spiffed up. Cozy. I'd even washed, carefully in the sink, Great-Aunt Bette's handmade lace curtains. After the collider people took possession of this property, I had to remember to pack those too. But we still had time, I told myself. A whole year.

I'd noticed Mel had even left his boots outside the back door. I was surprised, though, to hear behind me another voice from the kitchen. Then there was Steve, stepping into the living room, holding a bouquet of flowers.

"Guess I should have called first," he said. "I don't want to interrupt."

The two men stood, and I was surprised when Steve—after quickly thrusting the flowers into my hands—shook hands with each of them, calling them by name, Don and Dave. Names, I thought as I smiled down into the blue Gerbera daisies and white carnations, as interchangeable as the men's shirts.

"I swung by the hospital to give you these but you were already gone," Steve whispered to me. "I'm only just finding out. Are you okay? Can you walk?"

"My niece tried to outrun a rattler," Mel explained to Don and Dave. "But snakes always win, don't they, Steve?"

Steve glanced at Mel. All four men wore the same tight, thin-lipped smile.

I took the flowers to the kitchen and looked under the sink for a vase. I heard the men say they didn't want to take up much of Mel's time. Steve offered to pack up the last of his father's tools in the barn, but Mel told him he might as well stay.

There was, I knew, the promise of big money on the papers the men were passing around when I returned, standing in the doorway, perched like a strange bird on one leg, the good leg. Big money. And it was none of my business.

I stood in the doorway with the vase of flowers. I'd been thinking. I'd been talking on the phone to Marlene, thinking aloud: a town like Bozeman could maybe use a store like the Chef's Pal. It wasn't crazy, *was* it? Was *I*?

Steve motioned to me to come and take his seat, but I shook my head. He smiled at me, and I saw the softness. He hadn't come to pack anything. All his father's things were gone. He'd come to see me.

Negotiated Settlement

I'd been wrong—dead wrong, foolhardily wrong—about the big money I thought Don and Dave were signing over to Mel. No. The supercollider people were rescinding their offers—to us Lundstrums and to Steve's family, the Seversons. Just as Steve had predicted, they'd found the ground deep down too porous. Mel was pleased. Steve shrugged and said his family had had that land for a hundred years, and he guessed they could hang on to it for a hundred more. It had been paid for, a dollar an acre, in 1906.

Now, like some strange cross between a marriage counselor and a realtor, I was working out the terms of a deal between Dot and Mel. Currently on the table was the proposition that Mel would head back to Spokane in mid-October: before the snows came and he had to stop work on the excavations anyway. He would button up the house, winterize it, shut off the water. Then, come mid-April, he could come back, if he still wanted to. He could stay all summer.

"So if we all get agreed on this, then you can scoot," Mel said to me. "Right?"

I limped over and hugged him, pleased there might finally be resolution. "I should get out while the getting's good—that's what you're saying, I know. And I have to tell you, I agree. Most of me agrees."

He squeezed me. "Jessie loved you," he said. "Like a sister." I felt him catch his breath. His beard stubble brushed my forehead.

We sat down on the porch step, where we'd taken to watching the barn owl every night, hunting at dusk. "Remember that time she and I went to Florida?" I asked.

"Right. To visit Aunt Mary and her girls."

"Is Mary still married to that Coast Guard guy?"

"Lord no, that's been over for years. We still get a card every Christmas, though, from that older one, Deidre. She's a nurse now. In Miami."

I smiled and breathed in deeply. A nurse. I hadn't heard that. The owl's wings were loud—the sound of wet towels being shaken. We could hear him take off long before we could see him.

"I forget what became of the younger one—married, I think—but she landed on her feet too." Mel nodded to himself.

"Jessie will too," I said. "I'm not giving up on her. I'm not."

"She was worried we'd all be ashamed of her."

"I wish I'd seen what was happening *sooner*. I keep thinking if I'd understood, I could have done something."

Mel put a hand on my shoulder. His eyes when I looked into them were rimmed with tears. "Why do you think she'd go such a bad way? I wonder about that day and night."

"It was all around her and she just slipped." I felt a cool tear slide down my warm cheek. "She just fell into it."

He pulled a blue paisley handkerchief from his back pocket and handed it to me. "It's clean," he said.

The owl came toward us from the river. It was carrying a still-wriggling something in its claws. The wingspan must have been a good six feet. Then I realized that wasn't the barn owl; it was a great horned owl.

"I think ordinary life was of no interest to her." Mel watched me dab my eyes. Then he shook his head. "I hate to see you aggravate your eyes. Honestly, Lynnie, between those eyes of yours and now that gimped-up leg."

"I know," I said. "I can't decide if I'm more ridiculous or pathetic."

Mel set both his palms firmly on his knees. "Well, now, I'm not sure it has to be one or the other."

The Thing Is

"The thing is, I love my kid," Steve said. It was a statement that just hung flatly in the air among the fireflies, insects we rarely saw in Montana.

Mel and I sat with our hands in a tub of dirty water. We were waiting, I guess, for Steve to say more. But he was gazing off toward the brilliant but bruised-looking edge of the sunset.

"Well, that's right," Mel said finally, since it seemed that someone had to say something.

"For the last year I've been living across town from my wife, and every once in a while we visit this counselor guy who tells us perfectly good reasons we should have another go at it. But the truth is, the reasons only sound good up there in his office for twenty minutes. Back in our lives, in our real lives . . . I don't know . . . the reasons don't seem to match up with what's actually happening."

Steve said all this while staring down at a bone Mel believed was a piece of a fibula. We weren't making any guesses about a fibula of what, though.

"So you haven't had any other *go*'s, then?" I ventured. This seemed what he needed from Mel and me—some help with whatever it was he was trying to say. Mel shot me a look. *Don't pry,* the look said. But of course it was too late.

Steve shook his head. "We were supposed to talk with the counselor today, but I canceled."

Mel handed him a cloth to dry the piece of bone, but Steve just took the cloth and looked at it.

"It seems kind of nuts now," Steve said. "I mean, any more of those talks. It seems a long way in the past, that other life . . . now, now that I've started to have feelings for someone else." He glanced at me, then at Mel. Steve's face was impossible to read, a blank openness. He set the cloth down on the ground and put the bone shard on top of it.

Mel frowned and blinked. He turned to me. For a moment I felt accused of something. I sat cross-legged with Steve on my left and Mel on my right. A triangular force field around the washtub. Now they were both looking at me. I felt I'd been sucked into an enormous wave that was swirling me up and churning me around, and I had no clue if eventually there'd be a shore. I closed my eyes. Mercifully there was silence inside the wave.

Then I took a breath and reached my left hand out—out of the wave, and out of the pan of murky water my hand had really been in. The hot air met it, buoyed it. I moved it slowly, my eyes still closed. My hand stretched into a darkened limbo and hovered there, damp. Then I felt Steve's hand meet it. There was a sudden grip, a warm clench. And when I opened my eyes, I could hear the grasses again, rustling against one another, and I could see the fireflies.

"All right, then," Mel said. "No one's getting any younger." He nodded toward the tub that was still loaded with mud and rock and bone. "I hope I'm not going to have to finish off these suckers by myself."

Head Case

Jessie, age 46, Banda Aceh, 2005

Large, loud birds. Hot, salty breezes. I kept drifting off, dreaming of snow. I felt I wasn't where I should be, but I didn't know where "should-be" was. Except, as I told the nurse, I believed it was cold there. In dreams I'd seen cedars, jagged mountain peaks, and deep snow.

In fairy tales, the one who looks back at you from the mirror is the one who possesses the heavy-duty, otherworldly secrets. That's how I felt about the one staring at me from the small mirror in the women's latrine. Her eyes flashed a potent mix of pity and loathing. She had cornrows—with beads!—in her auburn hair. A blue-eyed girl. Gazing at myself, I knew I looked ridiculous. One earring had been ripped from my ear, but the other one I kept touching: a silver-encircled blue stone dangling three tiny silver bells that jingled in the dark of Red Cross Tent 5. Somehow the strange earring was the one thing I felt was mine. Was me.

My finger nudging it nudges me quite awake. Bright moonlight streams in though the open tent flap. Soon I will get up and go with the older Tent 5 girls, who are from Scotland and speak a language I mostly understand, to feed spoonfuls of a mush the girls call cuss-turd into the mouths of several sad, ailing elderly survivors. These people have lovely black eyes and caramel hands. One has a dislocated shoulder, another a broken wrist; an ancient man named Win is newly missing three fingers on his right hand, which had already, years ago, lost the pinky. Now that hand ends in just a thumb.

The Scottish girls call me Peaches. It's the color nail polish I'm wearing. I have no idea how it came to be on my toenails. We look down at our feet and go silent as we pass tents 9 and 10, inside which are the dead and almost-dead. When the girls look at my toes, I know they are thinking, as I am, of the absolute absurdity of polish enduring here where so many lives have been washed completely away, or have washed back to us with broken skulls, missing legs.

"Peaches, your green-shirt lady still can't get with that custard," the girl named Jenna says as soon as we're inside the oldsters' tent. The woman has not taken off her green shirt—and won't . . . no matter what semi-cleaner one is offered to her. Now she's shaking her head *no, no, no* to the Swiss Red Cross man as he holds the plastic custard container down to her.

I slip it from his hand and kneel beside her. Did he really think she'd be able to open it on her own? I watch his legs move to the next person. He's new. He's still expecting hope, gratitude.

The woman points to her closed mouth and winces.

"Still," I tell her, "you need to eat." I fill a spoon with some of the gruel. She makes a face that anyone would recognize as "yuck," but she lets me put the spoon gently into her mouth. She closes her eyes as she lets her tongue move through the food. High-calorie sustenance. On the label its contents appear in a language no one here can read. The food, in a blue basket, dropped down to us from a helicopter. When the chopper turned and rattled back across the eerily quiet Andaman Sea, we saw the big red cross on its side.

We heard that people on other continents were worried we'd starve. But there are lovely little fish here. When the island people of Phang Nga say the fish names, I think they are singing. The fish wash up around the bodies. Amid the rubble there are small fires all day and fish on sticks, sizzling.

I forget myself. This is what I consider as my response to a question, a blank look, a rolled eye. But I keep mum.

Dr. Z says I should be glad to be alive. The way he looks at me when he says this makes me believe it. Or want to. Yesterday he stuck a Band-Aid on my navel, over two small gashes.

"Looks like you might have had a ring there," he says.

"A ring?"

"Yes, like a navel ring. A piece of jewelry."

This I do not remember. Nor do I remember running inland with the others. I don't recall grabbing hold of palm branches. But this is what they've told me. Hotel Bulbul is no more. *Kaput.* *Kaput* is what the kids say about the boats washed ashore and the cars atop the pile of sticks that had been their school. Standing near these sticks and smashed desks, the kids stare at a tattered soggy map of the world. The North Pole is kaput. The inks of many countries have bled into one another.

Cremation fires—embers and small flashes—carry on in the predawn hours. Waking, I feel so new to the world, I think this may be how it's always been.

This morning, on the Scottish girls' radio, we heard men explain shifting tectonic plates. The voices sounded smoothed over by facts: the quake's magnitude and from exactly how far below the sea it must have come to heave the water so high.

Jenna took a stick and drew lines and arrows in the sand while Karen and I stared down.

A breeze was already mussing up the idea at our feet.

"Yeah, I guess. Maybe," Karen said.

According to the radio men, a couple of microseconds have been shaved off the earth's rotation.

How to add that to the equation? *What* equation? Overhead, enormous gray clouds careen into chubby white ones. The pretty yellow-vented bulbuls sing and fly through them.

Lying on grass mats with blue sheets pulled up to their chins, the Scottish girls whisper in the dark. They think I'm sleeping when I'm not. *Dead to the world,* they say. *What a head case.*

Although the young Red Cross doctor claims to be Danish, he calls me Fraulein Peach. He asks, "Do you want to go home?"

"I don't know," I say.

"Think about it," he tells me. "The answer will come to you."

What comes to me is that I might have—as the person I used to be—mustered up a little crush on him. She would do that, I think. She was just that type.

I've been awake for three days, but before that asleep—comatose, I'm told—for two. I thought that maybe in another day or two I'd get hold of myself. I'd recall my town, which everyone was sure was in America. Because of my accent. Also, I didn't want to have to keep answering to Peaches. Tomorrow in Tent 1 there would be phones set up and no doubt a throng of people queued up to call families, to report in, to say they were safe. Although Hotel Bulbul on Khao Lak Beach was kaput, somehow these folks were alive. A wall of water had come over them but spared them. Day and night, I heard the word *miracle*. And I felt that, yes, surely there was someone I should call. This haunted me more than my missing name and my missing home. My people. Who were my people?

The nurse comes by and says she'll unbraid my hair and we can give it a good washing, better than the "cursory" one my head had while I was "blotto." I touch the shaved place where my ten little stitches feel like plastic netting.

"Maybe tomorrow," I say, which I realize is what I said yesterday to her same kind offer.

I learn about flocculation. Add the packet of aluminum sulfate, stir for five minutes, dump the water through the sand filter, and mix in the chlorine. The sweet doctor's hands show me how. *Voilà.* I can't say for sure, but I don't think whoever I was before would have done this.

"Peachy-girl," one of the Scottish girls shouts, "can you catch the rugby kid?"

The kid in the rugby shirt three sizes too big for him has run into the old folks' tent again. He's a fireball, that one. Always shouting and laughing, always looking for someone to play a game that involves a set of three small balls. The first time he held them up to me, I had no idea what to do. I tried to get him to throw one to me. I mimicked toss and catch.

He thought this was hysterically funny. He bent over laughing.

Then I dropped a blanket over his head of dark curls. That of course was a joke too, but when I jerked the blanket off, he just stared at me.

"Sorry," I said.

"Sorry," he imitated. Clearly he was ready to talk. He'd speak whatever language a person spoke to him.

"Peach-ezz," he says now and shows me the three balls again. Then he laughs and takes off running, passing Mr. Win, who aims the bandaged hand with its thumb out to stop the boy, but the boy is fast and just veers around Mr. Win.

"Stop," I call.

The boy turns, smiles at me, then waves and ducks under the closed tent flap.

I follow, thinking I'll make sure he gets back to his tent okay, to the other *dek dek*, the kids. But someone is already looking for him, a Thai girl, maybe eighteen or twenty. She yanks the boy's arm, not hard but authoritatively. *Ay Noo,* she calls him, which apparently is a word I know: *kid, boy kid.* How do I know this? How do I know this isn't his name?

As good as dead. That's what I overheard Karen tell Jenna about how they'd found me: covered with sand, conked out, with a pretty pink fish, more thoroughly dead, on my chest.

Tectonic plates. The earth shrugged.

Words. *Bulbul.* Words I don't know how I know.

I brush my teeth with a new purple toothbrush. The woman in the mirror raises an eyebrow at me. The jingle of my silver earring makes me smile at the one who frowns. The truth is, every day I feel less sure, not more, about who I am. My age, for instance. I could be thirty. Even forty. Jenna says if I were a dog, we could hazard a better guess. Her father's a veterinarian, and he's shown her how to check the wear on a dog's molars. The raised eyebrow has two gray hairs among the blonde ones. Did I wash up with these, I wonder?

What I do remember? I am told to concentrate on this.

This: how no one could walk away from the sea, how the sea came for everyone. The frothy white loveliness before one realized what the wave was, what it intended to do.

The retreating water: its suck, its roar, the flailing limbs, the rainbow of swirling fishes.

Men in yellow hardhats spraying disinfectant on the white-plastic-wrapped bodies.

Fires against the night skies, that backdrop of constellations—stars that feel cruel to me now, spiteful.

And the unnumbered tent. Its stacks of unfilled coffins. Waiting, waiting.

I head back to Tent 5, and there's the rugby boy pointing to himself. "Sun," he says, a pronunciation perhaps closer to *soon.* So he is named. I'm happy. And jealous.

Sun and I walk toward the oldsters' tent, passing the nurse, who wags a finger at my silly braids and shakes her head. The soap will hurt, I know, when it hits the stitched-up hole through which a part of me has leached out.

Then Jenna and Karen come out of Tent 12, crying. No one we know in there was supposed to die, so as soon as I see the girls' faces, I am crying too. Those are our charges in there. The girls take my hands.

I move to open the tent flap.

"No, Peach," says Jenna.

"Peach, no," says Karen.

"It's green-lady. Dr. Z says we should wait out here." Jenna wipes her face with her shirttail.

"Wait with us," Karen says. She squeezes my hand.

We wait. Sun squats by my knee. I'm wishing I'd stayed longer with the old woman, wishing I'd unloaded more spoonfuls of the awful gruel into her ravaged mouth. I feel a small, cool finger cross my big toe's nail, and when I glance down, I see that Sun is scratching off the few specks of color—like a light dusting of coral—that remain.

I nod. *Good.*

He scratches.

Now nothing remains.

Acknowledgments

Thank you, Philip Graham, Patricia Henley, and Anna Monardo, for your friendship, support, and encouragement. For suggestions on earlier drafts of these stories, a special thanks to Laurie Alberts, Sven Birkerts, the late Stanley Lindberg, and F. K. Loskot; and as always, for his steadfast care, advice, and assistance at every stage, thank you, Rik Nelson.

I gratefully acknowledge the editors of the journals in which the following stories, most in different versions, first appeared: "Head Case" was originally published in the *Kenyon Review Online*, and was also included in the anthology *Sudden Flash Youth: 65 Short-Short Stories*, edited by Christine Perkins-Hazuka, Tom Hazuka, and Mark Budman (New York: Persea Books, 2011). "Retro Xmas" first appeared in *Sou'Wester*; "A Kingdom Comes" in *Massachusetts Review*; "Never the Face" in *Laurel Review*; the "One-Eyed" sections, all under the title "Black Fields, Black Horses," in *AGNI*; "The Rage of the Bipedal" in *Colorado Review*; "Funeral of the Virgin" in *Georgia Review*; "The Wild Boys" in *High Plains Literary Review*; excerpts from "Boneland" in *Cutbank*; and "Galilee" in *Southwest Review*.

And thanks as well to the Christopher Isherwood Foundation for a fellowship, which helped toward the completion of this book.

CPSIA information can be obtained at www.ICGtesting.com
Printed in the USA
LVOW130410020713

340954LV00004B/8/P